DISASTER!

Not My Plan!

ENDORSEMENTS

In *Disaster! Not My Plan!* Readers grab backpacks and canoes for a second exciting wilderness adventure with Jan (also known as Jantastic). This time, Jan is an assistant leader at a camp for girls on a whitewater canoe trip. In addition to helping the girls learn to work together, Jan must come to terms with an unskilled leader who resents Jan's presence.

The author's first-hand knowledge of life in the wilderness, and Jan's reliance on prayer, God's Word, and the "Little Voice" of the Holy Spirit (even when plans go horribly wrong) make for an unforgettable adventure. I highly recommend this gripping story of a young teen struggling to make sense of God's love and care in a beautiful but dangerous environment.

—**Ann Cavera**, Author: *Ride a Summer Wind,* Podcast: "Speeding Past 80"

An entertaining and inspiring book filled with adventure, all the while reminding us we are never alone during the good and the bad times. I'm looking forward to sharing this with my grandkids someday.

—**Sandra Rydall**, Espanola, Ontario

An exciting, challenging adventure that takes 'Jantastic' through a roller coaster of emotions, determined to prove to others and herself that she is more than capable of handling any situation. Her strength, courage, and wit guide us through twists and turns that you're certainly not expecting, and keep you wanting more. Great read!
—**Karen Collins**, Dispensary Manager, Robinson's PharmaSave

Disaster! Not My Plan! by P. Lynn Halliday is a heartwarming novel about God's sovereignty, even when life around us doesn't go as we expect. It follows the adventures of a group of girls on a canoe trip, and as they face one setback after another, readers learn the truth that God is worthy of our trust. This charming story leaves the reader with the reminder that sometimes the best adventures are found in God's unexpected plans.
—**Carol Schlorff**, Author: *How to Kill a Giant* and *How to Make a Miracle*

Lynn Halliday knows her God, and she knows a Grumman too. An adventure with a faith lesson for young adults.
—**Claire O'Sullivan**, author of *Romance Under Wraps, Silk & Slipper, Shanghai Road*, & the sci-fi, genetic engineering thriller, *Rules of Engagement*

DISASTER!

Not My Plan!

P. Lynn Halliday

A Christian Company
ElkLakePublishingInc.com

COPYRIGHT NOTICE

Disaster! Not My Plan!

Cover and Interior Design: Kelly Artieri, Deb Haggerty
Editor: Paula Peckham, Cristel Phelps, Deb Haggerty

PUBLISHED BY: Elk Lake Publishing, Inc., 35 Dogwood Drive, Plymouth, MA 02360, 2026

Library Cataloging Data
Names: Halliday, P. Lynn (Lynn Halliday)
Disaster! Not My Plan! /P. Lynn Halliday
308 p. 23cm × 15cm (9in × 6 in)
ISBN-13: 9798891344983 (paperback) | 9798891344990 (trade paperback) | 9798891345003 (e-book)
Key Words: Christian middle grade fiction girl adventure; Religious fiction 12-year-old fear friendship; Faith-based middle grade outdoor action humor; Christian values fun fiction girl canoeing animals; God values middle grade fiction family friends; New girl school adventure river Jesus love hope; Values virtues perseverance Christian girl fiction
Library of Congress Control Number: 2025951571 Fiction

DEDICATION

This book is dedicated to my husband Bob—my partner in adventure for over forty-nine years. Even in my camp leadership days, he was there to enable and encourage me and is here now to remind me of dates and the minute details of the escapades of my youth. It has been an exciting journey—may the adventures continue until the end.

ACKNOWLEDGMENTS

I would like to mention the very professional help I have received from Elk Lake Publishing, especially from my direct editor—Paula Peckham. Thank you for your patience and hard work. In addition, I would like to thank my beta-readers, Sandy Bousquet and Karen Collins, who encouraged me enormously with their kind words.

CHAPTER ONE

"I can't believe this is the last portage on our trip." I leaned my canoe against the fork of a tree. Sweat flowed into my eyes while I took a moment to enjoy the sight. "The portages may be grueling on the Mattawa River, but you sure can't beat the view." Tall rocky hills surrounded this river, giving it a wild, untamed appearance.

My older brother, Brad, dumped his pack on the ground and came to stand beside me. "You're sure right about that, Jan. The Mattawa River beats the Sauble River every time when it comes to sights, and billy-goat paths that pretend to be portages." He grinned, flexing a bicep. These trails didn't daunt him—he was always ready for a challenge, the harder the better. "Well, Sis, enough standing around. We're burning daylight." He laughed when I rolled my eyes.

I positioned myself under the canoe again and lifted it off the branch. "Ahhhhh, are you behind me, leaning on the canoe, Brad? It feels way heavier now." Brad's laughter floated from somewhere up ahead. "Wow, how'd he get that far away so quickly? I better catch up or I'll never hear the end of it." I shifted the canoe to a more comfortable position on my shoulders and peered ahead to locate the trail. "There it is."

I was always amazed at how little I could see while portaging a canoe, so finding the trail was a big deal. Trudging along over rocks and tight curves, I began to doubt my choice of paths. This section of the path was even rougher than the other one. "Man, imagine them having the nerve to call this a portage."

Groaning, I moved along the trail anyway. "Strange, the path seems to head away from the river—there must be some large obstacle they had to go around." Choosing each foothold carefully, I rounded the next bend, slowing down even more to survey the tree-lined path ahead. "Hmmm, looks a bit narrow, but it must be possible, since this is the portage." I marched forward and jammed my canoe between two trees on the trail. "Hey, I'm stuck—canoe, you need to go on a diet." I chuckled and backed up, but missed the original path by a few feet, lodging my load between two new trees behind me. "Rats, stuck again."

Frowning, I yanked the canoe from between the trees with all my might. It released suddenly, sending the canoe and me plunging over a ledge. I fell to my knees, then flat onto my face with the canoe landing on top. Pain shot through my shoulder as it hit the ground. "Ouch." Groaning, I tried to push the canoe off. It didn't budge. Sweat pouring from my face, I tried again. Trapped. Panic gripped me. "What if I'm stuck here forever?" Banging, pushing, kicking, I flipped over on my side, then onto my back. Exhausted, I panted, staring at the floor of the canoe.

"Face it, Jan, you're entombed," my inner voice said.

"Oh, calm down—remember you're an experienced tripper, now. Think logically," my mature self replied.

To which my inner voice retorted, *"You can't. You're not the logical one, you're the excitable one—there's only one course for you."*

I screamed. The sound echoed back to me, like I was inside a big drum. Listening for a response and finding none, I screamed again, kicking, rocking the boat like some wild banshee. Worn out, I slumped back onto the ground. "I'm doomed." Tears flowed.

Wait. Were those voices? "Help, help, help," I screamed.

The voices stopped talking.

"Oh, no, they've gone." I whimpered. "What now?"

"Have you forgotten about me?" asked Little Voice.

Perking up, I remembered. God was there—He always heard me. I squeezed my eyes shut. "Help me, Lord." I waited—mostly calm. Talking voices resumed—Dad and my older sister, Susie!

"Hey, Dad, did you hear something?" asked Susie.

"I think so. It came from somewhere to the right of us."

"I'm over here," I yelled. I drummed my heels against the floor of the canoe.

"Dad, you're right. I think it sounded like Jan. I'm going to follow this secondary trail and see if she's there. Jan? Jan, are you in trouble?" she yelled.

"Yes, I am, Susie. I'm stuck down a hill," I replied. "Thank you, Lord." Wiping the tears from my face, I waited for my rescue.

"Hey, Dad, I've spotted a canoe down the hill in front of me, and I think it might be Jan. Can you come and help?" yelled Susie. "Jan, I'm here. Are you okay?"

"Sure. I'm glad you found me. I'm trapped under my canoe."

Laughing in relief, Susie appeared at my side, her face peering under the edge of the canoe. "Hi there, Jan. That's an odd way to take a rest. Does this shelter protect you from the bugs? You always were the most creative one." She gave my shoulder a squeeze. "Dad's coming, and we'll have you out of there in a jiffy."

"Oh, the shame of it all. I'm never going to live this down—but then, there's nothing new about that." Shrugging, I sighed. "At least it wasn't Brad who found me."

Five minutes later, Dad and Susie lifted the canoe off me. They hauled me into a big hug. "Well, JanPan," Dad said, "this was an exciting end to our trip. You're always doing something memorable. Let's get going, we're ..."

"Burning daylight." Susie and I chimed in together, laughing as we looked at each other.

"Well, it's true, if we want to get home tonight," Dad mumbled, puzzled at our laughter.

We all shouldered our loads and headed off along the original portage trail. Brad sat on a stump by the river, fishing.

"Thought you'd never get here. What took you so long, Pipsqueak?"

"Oh, I lay down for a little rest along a side trail." I winked at Susie.

"Ya, she was using her canoe for a blanket when we found her," laughed Susie.

Brad wore a mystified expression.

Dad plopped their canoe beside ours and began loading it, whistling a little tune but saying nothing.

I quickly packed our canoe, giving Dad a quick grateful smile. I turned to Brad. "How far to the last set of rapids?"

Brad dropped the last pack into our canoe and strapped it in. "Just around the bend, up ahead," he replied. "We don't need to stop and look at these, Jan. There is a clear V at the top, indicating a chute. As long as you don't close your eyes, it should be a breeze."

I growled. "You know very well I'm over that fear now." I shot water in Brad's direction with a paddle. He ducked and grinned. He liked nothing better than to remind me of my foolishness a few years ago, where on a similar chute I had closed my eyes, thrown down my paddle, and screamed, "I don't wanna." I felt certain that story would show up at my wedding. Perhaps today's exploits would join the "embarrassing moments of my life" board? I crossed my eyes and stuck out my tongue. Paddling with my brother could be trying at times.

"Okay, you two. Quit the banter and shoot the chute," said Dad. But he couldn't disguise his amusement.

"Right, you are, Dad. Ready, Pipsqueak?"

"Always." I made the bow cut, and we plunged down the chute. "Whoopee," I squealed. Nothing was more fun than whitewater paddling. I glowed as we reached the endpoint of the trip.

"Great trip," I said. The words were echoed by all. Next stop, home. Then what? "I have no idea what adventures lie ahead this summer, but my life is never dull." Twirling, I dumped my load into the car.

CHAPTER TWO

I finished the last entry in my diary and lay back, chewing on the end of my pen while I reread the page. When you keep a diary, you want it to contain your deepest thoughts, your most important life stories, but you have to be accurate. Who knew if someone would want to make a movie of my diary someday, like they did with Anne Frank?

"Nah, who would make a movie of my life?" But I didn't care. I threw down my diary and pen and leaped to my feet. Twirling in a circle, I gave myself a pinch. This was real. I was home. Glancing around, I perused my room, then flopped onto the bed. I let my breath out slowly. Home never felt so good. "Strange, sometimes you have to leave something to realize it's important to you."

My face lit up. "Ooh, that's a mature, very profound thought." I grabbed my pen and added it to my diary—then tossed them back on the bed.

"Jan, where are you?" Susie peeked around my door, then dashed in—plopping onto the bed beside me. My pen jabbed her. "Ouch, I might have known the first thing you'd be doing was writing in that diary, but at least you're not still writing to that dumb donkey." She rolled over, dragging my diary out from under her.

"Gaston—" I snatched the diary from her. "—will always be my best friend, but I don't write to him anymore. I'm fourteen years old now." I huffed, lifting my nose in the air, but I couldn't help feeling a bit guilty—I did still keep in contact with Gaston. I stole a quick peek at Susie.

"Yes, you're very ancient, but are you telling the whole truth?" A sassy smile lit her face. "Didn't I see a letter set aside for Mom to mail, addressed to Mrs. Murphy?" Her eyes twinkled.

Indignation blazed through me. "Of course, you did. That's what friends do—they write to one another. Mrs. Murphy became my friend through years of writing Gaston. She's still living on the same farm as he is." Crossing my arms, I turned away.

"Oh, pardon me for thinking she still reads letters to Gaston like she used to. Glad to hear you're past that stage. You're still a little strange, you know."

She ducked when I launched a pillow at her. Laughing, she tossed the pillow back and got to her feet. "Well, I didn't come in here to tease you."

"So, why did you come in?"

"Mom told me to find you."

"Why?"

"I don't know. Go ask her. When you're done, come and get me. We'll find Brad and go for a hike." She sauntered out of the room with a wave.

I watched her go. We got along so well now, it amazed me. The sibling competitions had ended, and we enjoyed each other's company. I would miss Susie when she headed off to school in the fall. Our little 'down' time now was nice. We'd spent the week yakking with friends, neighbors, and even the local newspaper about the canoe trip. I gave my head a shake. Everyone wanted to know about the latest

McLean trip. No one else did neat stuff like that. We were like rock stars. I sat dreamily, picturing myself as a famous adventurer.

"Jan, are you upstairs?" Mom hollered. Even stars have to run when their mother calls. I jumped to my feet, practically right on top of Shad. "Sorry, Shad, I didn't see you lying there." Shad, our Australian sheepdog, usually lay close by when I was home. He wagged his tail when I scritchy-scratched his ears.

"Where's Mom?"

He bowed in a lazy stretch, then led me out the door. Shad took me straight to her in the living room. She waved as she hung up the phone.

"Hi, Mom, did you want to see me? What's up?"

"Hi, Jan. That was Mrs. Parker on the phone. She's got a problem I think you could solve, if you're feeling up to it."

"Sure, Mom, I feel fine. My bruises are gone, and I'm raring to go. Must be the wonderful meals you've been making. Canoe tripping food is great, but you can't beat comfort foods like mac and cheese." I smacked my lips, grinning.

"Glad to hear it. Well, here is Mrs. Parker's dilemma. The twins have contracted pink eye, and the daycare has asked their mother to keep them home for the rest of the week to give it time to clear up. Mrs. Parker can't get off work, and Mr. Parker is out of town for the week. She's asked if you'll babysit the twins."

I twirled. "Mom, do you realize what this means?" I threw my hands in the air, then hugged myself. "My first job—I'm an adult."

Mom turned away, covering her grin—unsuccessfully, I might add—with one hand. Clearing her throat, she asked, "Do you think you're up to the task? It's a lot of work caring for four-year-old twins. They're pretty active."

Putting my hands on my hips, I replied, "Piece of cake. I'm plenty active enough to keep up with them." I harrumphed. As if I, Jantastic McLean, couldn't outrun, outplay, or outsmart a pair of four-year-olds? "I'm going to ace this job, you'll see. Then babysitting jobs will pour in. Why, I'll make so much money I'll have to open up a bank account."

Mom grinned. "Well, if you're sure, I'll call Mrs. Parker and let her know. You'll need to start tomorrow morning at eight o'clock."

I scurried out of the room to gather the tools for my new job. I'd show them. Look out, world—here comes the best babysitter ever. Determination sizzled with every step.

"Are you sure you're starting out with the right attitude?" whispered Little Voice.

I skidded to a stop. Little Voice was back. That was the voice God used to get my attention. I shook my head. "Not now," I mumbled as I ran for my room.

My room had some amazing treasures in it. A "tickle trunk" full of costumes and neat, acting-related stuff; games; art supplies; and some great kid books. I yanked open my closet door and slammed it shut again. "Man, that was close." I had forgotten that before leaving for the canoe trip, I had sort of 'cleaned' my room—as per Mom's orders. "Rats. Now I really have to put stuff away, or I won't be able to find all my neat stuff." I smacked my head, mumbling, "Fluff for brains."

"Jan?"

I jumped. Mom stood behind me—a curious smile lighting her face.

"Yikes, Mom, you scared me. How long have you been standing there?"

"Long enough to watch you slam your closet door." She stepped around me and pulled the door open.

I grimaced, face reddening, as my treasures spilled into the room.

"I guess we both know what you'll be doing for the rest of the afternoon." Chuckling, she left the room. "Oh, by the way, you're hired," she called from down the hallway. Her laughter echoed back to me.

I sat surrounded by the pile of junk. "Not funny," I mumbled to Shad, who thumped his tail from somewhere under the pile. He didn't mind my mess. I crossed my arms, glaring at the door.

CHAPTER THREE

Dear Diary,

I probably shouldn't be writing this letter right now. I'm supposed to be cleaning my room. Mom discovered my haphazard cleanup job from before the canoe trip, and she's making me clean it now. Is it my fault I have so much neat stuff there isn't any room to store it all, even with a room of my own? I need a second bedroom. That would solve everything. Hey, maybe I can have Susie's room while she's away at university—but I suppose I'd have to give it back when she returned. Rats, that won't work.

Well, I'd better get cleaning. I'm sure Mom will be back to check on my progress. Uh-oh, I can hear her coming.

I threw down my diary and pen just in time. I was busy folding clothes when Susie peeked around the corner. "Good grief, Susie, I thought you were Mom." I relaxed.

"Wow, that's quite the mess." She waded through it to plop onto the bed. "How did you have time to make it? I saw you less than an hour ago."

"Oh, I had thrown all this stuff into my closet before the canoe trip, but I forgot, and it all fell out when I opened the closet door. Mom spotted it." I sighed as I stared at the humongous pile.

"Rotten luck. Hope she doesn't peek in my closet." She winked. "So what about our hike? Wanna come?"

"Nah, can't. I'm a working girl now, so I have to get this chore done today."

"Working girl, you? You're too young to work unless it's cleaning the toilets at church." Susie ducked as I launched a pillow at her.

"For your information, oh smart one, Mrs. Parker hired me to care for the twins, starting tomorrow."

"That's a very responsible job. Aren't you afraid to do it? What if something happens to the twins while you're watching them?"

"Like what?" I jumped to my feet and paced, carefully picking my way through the treasures scattered across the floor.

"Well, let me see. They're four-years old, so they can run, they can hide, they can crash down the stairs, they can turn on the stove, they can run outside and get hit by a car ..." Susie ticked each disaster off on her fingers.

"Okay, okay, I get the picture." I paced faster, head down. Sweat dotted my forehead.

Susie laughed. "Oh, chill out, Jan, I was teasing. I'm sure that none of those things will happen. Lots of kids your age babysit—it's really quite common. You'll be great. Well, it's a beautiful day, so Brad and I are going hiking. See you at dinner." On the way out the door, she called back, "You can always pray."

“Thanks, maybe I will.”
“That’s a good idea,” said Little Voice.
This time I nodded.

CHAPTER FOUR

I sat still, staring at the pile in front of me. The new me remembered God was there and active in my life—hadn't the Disaster trip proven that? It seemed like yesterday Susie, Brad, and I tackled the Sauble River all on our own. I still couldn't believe we went over a waterfall, lost our canoe, injured Susie, and had a bear chase us—all before we made it to the rendezvous spot. That's when we realized God wasn't just a guy in the sky but was real and active in our lives. So why then was it so difficult to remember to pray?

With a sigh, I tackled the job in front of me. Fourteen-year-olds weren't supposed to have such deep concerns. I shrugged. A babysitting job was nothing worth praying about, not really. This was no big deal—watching the twins would be a breeze. Susie was trying to scare me. I chuckled. She'd managed it, but I wasn't going to tell her that. Shaking my head, I folded clothes and put away the scattered doodads in earnest. I scooped up my half-finished puzzle, stuffed it back into its box, then checked the floor. Empty at last.

"Ta-da," I whooped, leaping to my feet. "Now, it's time for business, Shad." He wagged his tail. "What shall I take, boy?" I walked into the clean closet to find my babysitting supplies, excitement tickling my belly. This would be fun. Imagine being paid to play all day.

Spying my hoarded Lego blocks, I yanked the box off the shelf. “Legos will provide hours of fun, probably a whole day of castle building.” Scooping up a pair of knights, I practiced a make-believe battle—defeating the black knight with a swish of my sword. “Take that, you dastardly villain.” I laughed with glee, glancing quickly around to see if anyone spied on me. I gathered a few horses and more action figures. That should do it. Now what? “Art, of course. What do you think, Shad?”

Shad, freed from the clothes pile, had moseyed over to plop down at the closet door. He thumped his tail, then pulled himself to his feet and padded off. “I wonder where he’s going?” I pulled out the markers, crayons, and charcoal, plus a stack of paper. Reaching for a box, I dumped the art things inside, then added the Legos.

I turned when an odd sound caught my attention. Shad ambled over to drop a ball in my box. I laughed as I scritchy-scratched his ears. “Thanks for the contribution. Did I forget the most important toy?” Satisfied, he gave a good shake.

I continued my search on the remaining shelves. “Ah, there they are.” Reaching way down to the bottom shelf, I pulled out a stack of picture books and a few tubs of Play-Doh. “That should do it.” I tugged everything out of the closet and dragged the box down the hall to the front door. Skipping, I headed off to find Mom. I wanted her to see the neat stuff I was taking to the Parkers’s.

“Hey, Mom. Where are you?” I shouted.

“In the kitchen,” she replied.

I bounded to the kitchen, my nose twitching—something smelled wonderful. My mouth watered. “When’s lunch? I’m starved. Cleaning is an exhausting job.”

"Tell me about it," Mom said, winking. "Yes, lunch is ready. Where are the others?"

"They've gone for a hike. Would you like me to check outside and see if they're close by?"

"Yes, please."

I scurried off. Yanking the front door open, I ran straight into Brad, who was reaching for the knob. *Whoosh.* I fell backwards, landing on my bottom. Picking myself up, I said, "You must have been in a rush. Did you smell lunch?"

A smile replaced the startled look on his face. "Nope, I didn't smell it, but it sounds great. I'm starved. We climbed up to the ridge behind the house. Probably the last bug-free climb before we get swarmed this spring. Hey, Susie, hurry up," Brad yelled. "Lunch is ready." He shouldered past me, heading for the kitchen.

I waited at the door for Susie. "Hi, you seem tired."

"I am," she sighed. "Remind me never, ever to go on a hike with Brad. He marches instead of walking, and every hill and ridge is a challenge he must try. I ask you, what normal person would go over a rock instead of around it, where possible?" She leaned with a heavy sigh against the doorframe.

I laughed as I helped her into the house.

Bending down to take off her runners, she noticed my box. "What's all this stuff?"

"Oh, just a few supplies I gathered to entertain the twins."

She peeked inside. "Hmm, that should prove interesting." She wore an inscrutable expression. I frowned at her.

"Let's eat," she said with twinkling eyes. Susie headed for the kitchen, calling, "Smells good, Mom."

I followed, concern settling in my belly.

CHAPTER FIVE

Dear Diary,

Well, today is the day. My first day at my first job ever. I guess I'm all grown up now. After all, a person wouldn't leave twins with an immature kid, now, would they? I'm a bit scared, probably because Susie planted disaster pictures in my head about all the things that could go wrong, but I've prayed about it and now I feel ready to face the challenge.

"Good job," said Little Voice.

I continued writing.

I've found the best stuff to bring along, too. Legos, art supplies, books, and Play-Doh. Even a ball donated by Shad. I have a feeling Susie thinks there is something wrong with this stuff, but she wouldn't say. She just gave me her I know best look. Well, I'm not worried. I've got this.

"*Who's got this?*" asked Little Voice.

The morning had arrived. I sprang into the kitchen with a triumphant "Ta-da."

Mom was there.

"I'm all ready for work. Do you think I need to bring a lunch?"

"Oh, good morning to you, too," laughed Mom. "Bringing lunch will probably not be necessary. I'm sure Mrs. Parker has organized the food for the day."

"But, Mom, how will I know how to make whatever she leaves me?" I plopped down at the kitchen table, chewing my lip.

"I'm sure Mrs. Parker will tell you what the twins like and how to make it. Just relax, Jan, you'll do a fine job, I'm certain of it." She gave me a big hug. "Now, eat up. You'll need your strength."

"Why? I'm not running a marathon or climbing a mountain. I'm just going to play all day."

Mom glanced at me. "Well, perhaps it will be more exhausting than you think."

"Mom, they're only four. I should have no trouble keeping up with them. I am fourteen, after all." I put my nose in the air.

"Perhaps you're right. I'd forgotten how mature you are. Well, have a good day." She turned away, grinning.

I'd had just about enough of everyone's negativity. I stomped out of the room, grabbed my box and headed across the street. I'd show them. I knocked on the door.

The door opened, and two children ran screaming out of the house. "Oh, my—excuse me for a second." A flustered Mrs. Parker raced after her twins. Two minutes later, she returned with one squirming kid under each arm. Setting the twins down, she said, “Children, I’d like you to meet Jan. She’ll hang out with you for the next few days. Pay close attention to everything she says. Jan, this is Gordie, and this is Donnie. Fondly nicknamed Thing One and Thing Two.” She ruffled their hair as she let them go. They were off like a shot.

“Wow, they’re fast, aren’t they? Should I follow them?”

“No, they’ll be fine. That was the playroom they’ve just entered. Let’s go to the kitchen. I’ve made a list of things to watch for and left you the number where I can be reached if needed.” She started down the hall but stopped when she noticed the box I held. “What’s in there, Jan?”

“Just a few supplies to amuse the boys. I used to spend hours playing with Legos, so I thought they might enjoy it, too.”

She glanced into the box. “Interesting. I guess we’ll see.” She grinned, then shrugged as she headed off.

I scooped up my box and followed. Entering a large kitchen, I discovered the room littered with discarded toys. “Oh. I thought the playroom was that way.” I pointed across the hall.

“It is.” Mrs. Parker stepped with precision through the toys to the kitchen table. “Here’s the list I mentioned. I’m sure it covers everything.” She checked the time. “Oh my, I’m running a bit late.” She dashed out the door and up the stairs to get ready for work.

I watched, uncertainty sinking into my mind as I reviewed the mess in front of me, then scanned the list in my hand. Suddenly, screams echoed from the playroom, grabbing my attention. The page fluttered to the floor. “I guess I’d better go see what they’re up to.”

I followed the sound with reluctance. Chaos greeted me when I entered the playroom. “Wow, and Mom thought my room was bad," I mumbled. The twins were busy playing tug-of-war with a pillow, screaming as they tugged. I gulped, then, putting my box down, I strode into the fray.

"Hey, boys, let's find another activity—one we can share," I said in my best mature voice. They paused, then dove onto the couch. Laughing with glee, they bounced up and down. I stood, unsure of what to do. "Now what?"

Mrs. Parker arrived and surveyed the scene before her with total disregard. "I see you've found the playroom. I expect you'll spend most of your time here. The boys enjoy going outside, so we also have a fenced-in backyard for them to play in. If the weather is fine, you'll also want to spend some time there."

"Do they go outside often?"

"Yes, they need to go outside to use up some of their endless energy."

I laughed. "How energetic can four-year-olds be?"

She smiled at the bouncing twins. "Oh, you'll find out."

I glanced with longing at my box filled with quiet play activities. An uneasy feeling crept over me. Maybe these things wouldn't work with "the boys." I shivered. Perhaps babysitting wasn't quite what I expected.

My daydream ended like a burst bubble as Mrs. Parker grabbed each squirming child to kiss them goodbye, then dashed down the hallway and out the door. I was on my own. Sweat gleamed on my brow.

CHAPTER SIX

Forcing a smile on my face, I turned. Shock—they were gone. Yikes, this wasn't good. "Hey, boys, where are you?" Rotating in a circle, I focused on listening. Not a sound. I walked down the hallway towards the entryway. The long, narrow space was the only neat and tidy spot I'd seen so far.

"Hmmm, they must have some rule about keeping the junk out of the hall." Shrugging, I continued my search, poking my head into each doorway I passed. "Now, let me see, I've checked the kitchen, the playroom, the den, and no sign of Thing One and Thing Two. I guess I learned one thing—why they're called that."

Grinning, I continued onward until I came to a set of stairs. "I wonder if they're up in their bedroom?" I tiptoed up the stairs. Maybe I'd catch them—I figured they were playing hide-and-go-seek, without bothering to tell me we were playing a game. "Ah, kids with imaginations. Just like me."

Nearing the top of the steps, I stopped to listen. Silence. "Hmmm, pretty strange, there's no giggling or whispering."

Kaboom.

I jumped. The echo of the blast hung in the air. I flew to the nearest window and spotted the boys peeking from behind a tree fort. Smoke drifted up from a barrel in the backyard. Their faces were pasty white as they clung to one another. I yanked open the window and hollered, “Stay there, boys—don’t go any closer to that barrel.” Leaping down the stairs two at a time, I dashed out the back door, screeching to a stop in front of the miscreants. “What have you been doing?” I glowered at them, hands on hips, toe tapping.

“Uh, we wanted to surprise you,” said Donnie.

“Ya, Jan, we wanted to show you how happy we are that you’re here,” added Gordie. Two hopeful faces peered up at me.

I melted. “Thanks.” I scooped them into a big hug. “So, what did you blow up?” Puzzled, I gazed around. Bits of wood, a few old cans, and lots of blackened soot littered the area around the barrel. “And how did you do it?”

The twins shuffled their feet, staring at the ground.

“Well?”

“I’m getting cold. Can we go in now?” asked Donnie.

“Nope, not until you tell me what blew up. I might have to call your mom if you destroyed something important.”

“No, no,” they yelled in unison. They darted glances at each other.

“We blew up a rocket,” whispered Donnie.

“A rocket?” Hands on head, I looked to the heavens. Could this be happening?

“Ya, one Dad bought for Victoria Day,” added Gordie. Excitement overrode their reluctance to ’fess up, and they jumped up and down, warming to the subject. “Daddy said he had a surprise for us and showed us the rockets.”

“Daddy promised to shoot them off next week. He has a big box full.” The boys quivered, eyes sparkling.

“We came to the backyard to play hide-and-go-seek,” said Donnie.

"We were searching for a spot to hide when I spotted the fire stick that starts the barbecue grill, and I got the idea to surprise you with fireworks." Gordie's face glowed with pride.

"I thought shooting one would be okay," said Donnie, nodding.

"Ya, and I figured if we put it in the barrel, then it wouldn't hurt us," added Gordie.

I narrowed my gaze. "Did your dad tell you it was okay to shoot one off by yourselves?"

The jumping stopped—heads hung down.

"He told us not to touch them," said Donnie. A tear fell, and sniffling began.

"He won't be happy we disobeyed," added Gordie, worry etched on his face.

"Why do you think Dad told you not to touch the rockets?" I asked.

"'Cause they're dangerous," both boys chimed in.

"Ya, I was pretty scared—the rocket flared when we lit it," said Donnie, eyes popping.

"I hid my face behind you," admitted Gordie.

"We both jumped behind the fort," said Donnie, "so we didn't get hurt." An appeal for understanding filled his face.

"Well, boys, I think the Lord protected you from harm. Did you learn anything?"

"Not to stand too close," said Donnie.

"Maybe to wait for Dad to do it," added Gordie. Two heads nodded in unison.

I smiled. "This event is over. Let's go inside and play with the Legos." Both boys leaped in the air, whooping—shooting off like rockets themselves for the back door.

"Wow, they sure move fast." I sprang after them, instincts kicking in—I needed to keep them in sight. On their own, they were sure to get into trouble—double trouble—Thing One and Thing Two. What an understatement that proved to be.

CHAPTER SEVEN

The door slammed behind me. I dropped onto the couch, groaning.

"Oh, Jan, you're home. How nice." Mom raised an eyebrow at my dishevelled appearance. "Yikes. Have you been through a war?"

I was a disaster. Marker hearts shone on my cheek, little elastics littered my hair, and my jeans were ripped.

I moaned. "Mom, a human sacrifice could not have suffered as much as I have today." I flung one arm over my face.

Mom put her hand over her mouth, eyes crinkling.

"It's not funny. They're monsters, creatures from the underworld, that have been allowed to escape and are now creating a menace. Lock the doors—so they can't invade our home."

"Ha, ha, ha, ha."

"No, truly, Mom. It isn't funny. They're one hundred percent uncontrollable—aptly named Thing One and Thing Two. How does Mrs. Parker stand it?" My eyes popped open in horror. "Was I like that?"

"No, dear, you weren't. Mrs. Parker is doing the best she can with her hyperactive twins. She's on her own most of the time because Mr. Parker works out of town, but I hadn't realized they were that bad."

"Bad?" I leaped to my feet. "Bad does not begin to describe it." I paced, getting more worked up as I circled the room. "They touched or threw everything that was not nailed down. When I tried to calm them down by drawing, they drew all right—on every surface that was *not* paper, including me. I tried everything I could think of—even Play-Doh, which, by the way, now decorates the playroom ceiling. When I asked them to model something, they told me they wanted to make a cave with stalactites. They wet the Playdough so it would stick and tossed it at the ceiling. How did four-year-olds even learn how to do that, I ask you?" I stopped pacing. "But the worst thing ever was they used my precious Legos as missiles in the 'War of the Twins.' My favourite, most guarded Lego kit is now scattered all over Mrs. Parker's house." I stopped in front of Mom, chest heaving.

"Just relax." Mom patted the seat cushion next to her. "Come and sit beside me."

I flopped onto the couch and put my head in my hands. "The house is a disaster—how will Mrs. Parker ever clean it up? I was a horrible babysitter." Tears streamed down my face.

"Oh, Jan, I'm sure Mrs. Parker has seen messes before. She knew you were inexperienced and was willing to accept you anyway. Were you fired?"

"No, she walked in the door, sent a calm glance around the room, and said nothing." I hung my head.

"What happened then?"

"The twins came running to give her a big hug. They told her I was the best babysitter ever, and they had so much fun." I hiccupped, catching my breath. "She smiled at me, Mom."

"Then you did the job that was most important to her."

I lifted my tear-stained face. "What job was that?"

"You loved and played with her children. She didn't hire you as a housekeeper. She hired you as a caregiver, and it appears you managed to do the job. Congratulations. So, what will you do tomorrow?"

I shot off the couch. "You mean I have to go back?"

"Why, of course, Jan. You promised to babysit for three days."

"But how can I survive this ordeal?"

"This time, don't go armed with toys. Go armed with God. Pray earnestly for love, understanding, and the wisdom to manage whatever situation comes your way." Mom patted my shoulder as she headed for the kitchen to make dinner. I watched her go, numb.

"Mom has the right idea. Come to me and I will give you rest," said Little Voice.

I sat down to pray.

CHAPTER EIGHT

Early the next morning, I marched across the street. I knocked, pasting what I hoped was a determined smile on my face. The door opened with a whoosh, and two hooded banshees leaped out to hug me. Peeling them off, I walked into the house.

"Good morning, Mrs. Parker."

"Good morning, Jan. You seem well-rested. I thought perhaps you might not return after your busy day yesterday. You were a bit dishevelled when you went home." She gave me a warm smile.

"I was exhausted. Honestly, Mrs. Parker, I don't know how you do it. How can you be so serene when the twins are so active?" The twins had attached themselves once again to my legs. I ruffled their hair.

"Gordie, would you get the box from the living room, please? Gordie ran off. Donnie stayed. "Let's go into the kitchen and have a little talk." She walked down the hallway. I followed, dragging Donnie. "Have a seat, Jan."

She put a mug of steaming hot chocolate in front of me. "Donnie, would you like some hot chocolate, too?" He nodded. She made two more cups, placing one at each of the kids' places at the table. Gordie arrived. After dropping his load on the floor, he joined us at the table. She patted his shoulder. "Thank you, Gordie."

Each child slurped his drink with a happy grin. Puzzled, I asked, "Why are they so calm?"

Mrs. Parker sat down to enjoy her cup of coffee, smiling with fondness at her twins. "Let me share something with you about the twins, Jan. With my endless work, and Mr. Parker's absences, my boys do not get much opportunity to play with other children. They often have to amuse themselves because I am so busy. Yesterday was the first time in a month they had someone new to play with. I'm afraid I set you up unknowingly."

Startled, I asked, "How so?"

"Well, I told them the night before they would have a new babysitter for a few days—someone young they could play with." She grinned. "Unfortunately, that wound them up, so by the time you arrived, they were pretty excited."

I grimaced. She laughed, eyes twinkling. She turned a questioning gaze toward the boys.

Taking the cue, Donnie said, "I'm sorry I didn't do everything you told me to yesterday." He hung his head.

Gordie hung his too then peeked up at me. "But we had soooooo much fun, didn't we, Donnie?"

"It was the bestest day we've ever had." Both boys held their breath, watching me with eyes full of hope.

My heart melted. Perhaps today would be bearable after all.

Gordie jumped up to fetch the box that he had dragged in. "Look, Jan, we found all of your Legos." With a shy glance, he handed me the box. Anticipation glowed in his eyes.

"Thanks, Gordie and Donnie. It must have taken you hours to find all those pieces." I took the box, lovingly running my fingers through the contents. "Hey, boys, do you want to build a castle?"

They leaped from the table. Whooping, they raced for the living room. "We'll get the other stuff." Happy laughter floated down the hall.

I grinned at Mrs. Parker. "I guess they do." Shrugging, I followed the boys, an unexpected spring in my step. "Have a nice day at work," I called over my shoulder. "I think this day will go much better."

Mrs. Parker headed out for work. I walked to the living room. As the door closed, I thought I heard her humming a little tune. Smiling, I entered the room.

I stopped in confusion. The twins had put a blanket on the floor and had made a sort of canopy above it. Like a cave. "What's up, boys? I thought we were building a castle."

"A castle is really big, isn't it, Jan?" asked Donnie. He tilted his head.

"Yeah, and the Legos are really small, right?" added Gordie. He tilted his head.

I stared at the two puzzled faces. Then understanding dawned. "Oh, I get it. What a creative idea, guys. The blankets are the outside walls and roof of the castle. Is that what you had in mind?"

They bounced to their feet to do a happy dance, then dove back into the "castle," not cave. "Can we make the castle buildings now?"

"Sure, you do that, and I'll find the knights and horses." I grinned.

"Don't forget their spears," Donnie said.

"Don't forget their helmets," Gordie added.

"I won't. Let's start playing, boys." The sound of happiness filled the house for hours.

Later in the afternoon, the door opened softly. Mrs. Parker entered a house filled with eerie quiet.

Putting my fingers to my lips, I indicated the peaceful, sleeping boys, snuggled close beside me on the couch. A movie played in the background with the volume turned low.

Puzzled, she stared at me, then her eyes scanned the room. The space was in perfect order, not a pillow out of place. Shock radiated from her face.

I grinned. Mission accomplished. *"Thank you, Lord,"* I whispered.

CHAPTER NINE

Dear Diary,

Well, I've had an interesting time since my last letter. I got a job as a babysitter. Can you imagine me, a babysitter? Well, I can tell you I am the bestest babysitter ever. I was told that by the twins, Donnie and Gordie. Mrs. Parker said she has never seen her boys so happy and well cared for and has never come home to such a clean house. The first day was a disaster, but Mom reminded me to pray before going back, and the rest of the days were great. I had forgotten how helpful prayer can be. I'm never going to forget to start all my projects with prayer—hold on, Diary, Mom's calling.

"Yes, Mom?" I hollered down the hall.

"Jan, you have a phone call."

"Come on, Shad." We ran to the kitchen, and I picked up the phone. "Hi," I gasped, out of breath.

"Hi, Jan, this is Ralph, the ABK camp director. I wondered if you'd be interested in helping with a junior canoe trip we're planning two weeks from now? The original junior leader has broken her ankle and is unable to come."

"Gee, Ralph, I'd love to help, but aren't I a bit young to be a leader?"

"Normally, yes, but you've had a lot of canoeing experience with your family, and we need someone with expertise. The senior leader has had lots of leadership and outdoor experience but has not done much canoe tripping. Together, you should make a good team."

I clasped the phone to my chest, eyes bulging. This was a dream come true. It couldn't really be happening. I took a deep breath and cleared my throat. "Sure, I'd be glad to help. Are the campers very experienced, and where are we planning to paddle?"

"They have been on at least one canoe excursion, but this will be their first whitewater trip. We plan to do a small portion of the South Channel of the French River—to give them a taste of whitewater paddling. Have you ever done the French River?"

"No, I haven't, but we have paddled the Sauble and Mattawa rivers."

"Ah, good. That should've given you plenty of experience to teach the essential whitewater strokes. Okay, I'll put you down for the junior outpost camp in two weeks. Thanks." He hung up the phone.

"Whoopee." I twirled.

I jammed to a stop and gave Mom a sheepish grin.

"What's got you alight?" she asked.

"That was Ralph, the Camp Aush-Bik-Koong director. You'll never guess what he asked." Calming down, I waited.

"Now, let me see. Why would a camp director call you? Her eyes sparkled. "Could it be he wanted you to help at the outpost camp?"

My mouth dropped open. "How did you know?" I whispered.

Laughing, Mom gave me a hug. "He asked me first." She grinned.

I slapped my forehead. "Fluff for brains. Of course, he did. I'm only fourteen years old. He would have to ask your permission, right? Well, what do you think, Mom?"

"It sounds interesting. Do you think you can do it? Are you sure enough of your skills?"

"Sure, I can. I bet I've got more experience than all the other leaders at camp. People have been talking about my—our—exploits for years." My brow furrowed. "I'll prove my experience is sufficient." I drew myself up to my full five-foot height, head held high.

Mom regarded me calmly. "Well, I guess we will see."

I turned away, confused by the doubt in Mom's voice. "I've got to prepare. See you at supper." Dashing away, I headed for my room to think.

Dear Diary,

The camp director just called to offer me a position as a junior leader at the outpost camp. About time my skills are being recognized. I think Mom doubts I can do this, but I'll show her and everyone else. It will be Jantastic to the rescue again—no, make that Super-Jantastic. Babysitting was just the warm-up. Big events await. My skills are tuned and ready to go.

"Have you asked for help yet? Remember your decision to start every project with me?" Little Voice asked.

"Dinner is ready," called Mom.

"Okay, Mom, I'll be just a minute. I'm buried in my closet."

After a bit, Mom appeared at my bedroom door. She hesitated before entering my room. She found my bum protruding out of a container. Gear flew out of the box onto the floor. She ducked as a missile sailed past her head.

"Oops, sorry, Mom." I sat back on my heels, surveying the mess. "I've got an explanation for all this clutter, really I do." I shrugged sheepishly. "I'm preparing for camp. I have to get the proper gear selected and stuffed into a knapsack. Camp doesn't always have the things we need."

"Wow, you sound just like Brad. Didn't you mock him last year for doing the same thing?"

"Ouch." I grimaced. "That's true, but I did learn a few things from him. Don't tell him I said so. Like the value of these." I held up the fat sticks I'd been searching for.

"And what are those odd-looking sticks?"

"They're fat sticks, Mom, and they're amazing. You can use them to start a fire when everything, including them, is soaking wet. I saw Brad use them, and they worked really well." I plopped them into the sack.

Shaking her head, she leaned back against the wall, arms crossed.

That sent a signal. I sat up. "What's up, Mom?"

"I came in here to speak to you about your role on this trip. What did the director tell you about it?"

"Oh, it's going to be terrific." I bounded to my feet, ticking off the points on my fingers as I walked. "Number one—I'm going as a junior leader. Number two—I have way more experience than the senior leader, so I'll be her advisor. Number three—we're going to practice whitewater paddling. And number four—we'll be paddling on a new river." I stopped and twirled.

"What river?"

"The French River, South Channel. Have you ever paddled that one?"

"Yes, years ago, as a camper and then a second time as a junior leader, like yourself, and then one last time as a senior leader."

"Was it a fun river? Was it hard?" After a hesitation, chewing my bottom lip, I asked, "Were there any waterfalls?"

Mom swooped over to give me a hug. "No falls, Jan."

My shoulders sagged. "Phew."

"But there were some tough rapids. I thought your group of paddlers were pretty new to canoe tripping."

"They are, Mom, but that's why I'm going along. I'm experienced." I lifted my head. "Anyway, we're not planning on shooting the whole South Channel. The plan is to camp at the mouth of the French River, then practice our skills on the first set of rapids. I think we're planning to spend two days there, and then, we'll paddle to a bridge that crosses Wolseley Bay at Highway 528. Easy peasy."

Mom just stood there, saying nothing, a little frown creasing her brow.

"What's wrong?"

"I'm concerned that novices will still have trouble with the first set of rapids. If I remember correctly, it has a small chute, some very big rocks, and large standing waves—all probable sources of disaster for your new canoe trippers. Quite frankly, I'm surprised the director has chosen that river for beginners. Did he tell you why?"

"No, he didn't say. Is it deeper than the Sauble River?"

"Yes, I think it is. You've probably guessed the reason. Dad was saying the Sauble River is shallow this year because of the lack of rain. That's why Dad took you to the Mattawa River for the family outing this year."

"We sure couldn't take beginners to the Mattawa, Mom. The portages were brutal, and the whitewater was quite challenging. Do you have any advice to share about the French River?"

"Make sure you teach the girls to get out in a jiffy if they get stuck on a rock. I remember some very sneaky rocks that hid just below the surface."

"Thanks, Mom, I'll pass that along. Now back to packing."

"Nope, quit the packing for now and come to dinner." She smiled as we linked arms to head to the kitchen.

CHAPTER TEN

At last, the day had arrived. I'd packed my bags and was ready to go. I shoved my knapsack into the trunk, then jumped into the car beside Dad. I fidgeted and rubbed my hands together.

"Is that anxiety or excitement I see?" he asked.

"I guess a little of both."

"Are you anxious about leading or about getting lost and going over a waterfall?" He grinned.

"No point in worrying about waterfalls. There are none this time." I stuck my tongue out. "But I might be a little concerned about leading."

"Well, you're not the main leader, just a helper. If you view it that way, perhaps the tension will ease a bit. From what I've heard, the director thought you could show the others how to do some strokes."

I gave my head a quick shake. "Perhaps, Dad, but I think my role will be a little more involved than that—I'm going along as the 'expert consultant'."

"Oh?" Dad lifted his eyebrows.

"Let's get going. I don't want to be late."

"I'm sure it will turn out fine." He patted my knee and started the engine. Before long, we arrived.

The parking lot at camp was chaotic—filled with campers and parents, cars and luggage. Dad struggled to find a spot to drop me off.

"Look over there, by the chapel. That's my senior leader, Lauren. I've met her before, but I don't really know her. I guess by the time this camp is over, we'll know each other well. We're going to have such fun together." I leaped out of the car, forgetting to close the door in my excitement. "Oops, sorry, Dad." I giggled as I returned to shut the door.

Dad watched me with amusement. "Try not to bowl her over with enthusiasm."

"Who, me?" A gay laugh escaped as I twirled.

"Is that you being calm?"

"Yep, it's as calm as I get." I leaned against the car, regarding Lauren. "Did you know her camp name is Daisy? Strange name for someone who is so tall and lanky. I wonder how she got it? She doesn't appear to be a delicate flower." I whispered, winking at Dad. "Well, husky trippers like us can't be small, fragile little flowers, can we?"

"No, they have to be big and muscular, like you." He smiled as he examined my stature.

"Exactly." I struck a pose, flexing my biceps. Then laughed, because a five-foot-nothing, one-hundred-pounder could never seem imposing. "Well, I'm mighty on the inside."

"Ha." Dad ducked his head and hid his smile behind his hand.

I frowned, briefly. No one ever took me seriously. But they would after this week, because I was going to be a leader of an canoe trip. I shivered with anticipation. "I'm going over to say hi. I'll be back in a few minutes to get my stuff." I dashed off, leaving Dad shaking his head.

"Hi, Daisy. I'm Jan McLean."

"Hi, Jan. Good to see you—I think we've met before, a couple of years ago. Actually, come to think of it, I have a picture that Mopsy sent me of you and Chrissy beside your overturned canoe, water lilies decorating your hair." She grinned.

I grimaced. She would have to remember that little incident. It had happened on the first day of camp, two years ago, when Chrissy and I got stuck in a marsh and ended up falling out of the canoe. Mopsy, our leader, had snapped a picture. My face flamed.

"The incident was rather funny, and Mopsy told me it helped the girls settle in—a great icebreaker. Perhaps you could do it again for our canoe tripping group?" She winked and then, still chuckling, she turned to greet two other girls who had just arrived. I stomped away to get my gear.

Rats. That wasn't the impression I wanted to give the girls. I was here because I had expertise in canoe tripping that others did not.

"What impression do you want to give? Will it honor me?" asked Little Voice.

I shook my head. Surely it wasn't wrong to want to do your best? I reached the car and jerked open the trunk. Grabbing my bags, I tossed them on the ground and then slammed the lid. Dad jumped. He rolled down the window and poked his head out. "Something wrong?"

"Nah, just in a rush. Sorry for startling you."

"No problem, JanPan. Have you got all your gear?"

"Yes. Thanks for bringing me. Will you pick me up next Saturday, please?"

"Sure thing. And Jan, we'll be praying for you. Don't forget who's really leading this trip." With a wave, he headed home.

Now, what was that all about? I knew who the leader was. Daisy. But I was the best helper she could possibly have wished for. Just wait until she saw what I could do. I grabbed my pack and trudged off to register.

"Jan, oh Jan, are you forgetting about me?" asked Little Voice. *"Your dad didn't."*

"Huh?" I shook my head grumpily.

CHAPTER ELEVEN

After registration, I joined the outpost group at the docks. We gathered around Daisy.

"Hi, everyone, and welcome to Junior Outpost. We're going to have a blast this year. I've planned a fun and challenging canoe trip for you. But more about that later. For now, I want everyone to choose her partner, then go to the boathouse and get your gear. Off you go." The air erupted in giggling chatter as the girls set about their task.

I looked around for a likely partner—someone who could keep pace with me. Across the grass, I noticed a small but muscular girl about my size who seemed familiar. When she turned around, I recognized her. The girl's name was Paige. She went to my school but was a year younger than I was. "Hi, Paige. Do you have a partner yet?"

Paige whipped around. "Oh, hi, Jan, I thought I recognized your voice. I don't have a partner yet and would love to be yours."

Relief flooded my body.

"I've heard you've done quite a bit of paddling, but I've only paddled around at our cottage. With you as a partner, the others won't leave me behind." She giggled and visibly relaxed. I smiled as we walked together to the boathouse.

"I've done quite a bit of paddling," I said. "It's a favourite family pastime. As a matter of fact, we've only just gotten back from a canoe trip on the Mattawa River, which was wildly exciting. There were tons of rapids, but also a lot of portages—or what passed for portages. In reality, they were goat paths, steep, winding, narrow trails—way too tight a squeeze for seventeen-foot canoes. I got stuck several times and had to get help."

"Who rescued you?"

"Luckily, Susie and Dad came along before Brad noticed I was missing. So, I avoided being razzed."

Paige listened with interest as she chose a paddle and lifejacket. "My older brother likes nothing better than having to rescue me. We always spar with one another." She chuckled. "Just two weeks ago, our family went to our cottage for the spring cleanup, and it was my job to get the dishes and kitchen gear out of the storage barrel. We have one of those big old wooden barrels that are about the same height as you and me." She rolled her eyes. "Well, I had to use a stool to reach into it, and I'm sure you can picture what happened," she said, raising her eyebrows.

A vision popped into my mind. Her accident was totally the type of thing that always happened to me. I slapped my thigh, laughing.

Paige grimaced. "I ended up doing a handstand in the barrel—all you could see was my feet." She rolled her eyes. "Tom pulled me out, and as you can imagine, he bragged about it for the rest of the weekend." We grinned at each other. "Oh, I see the other girls have already got their equipment and have joined Daisy. You'd better grab yours."

"I don't need to—I've brought my own." I indicated my paddle and lifejacket.

"That sure is a nice paddle."

"It's a black walnut Ottertail." I held it up, turning it over to show off the deep grain. "It's made special for whitewater paddling, with a long, narrow blade that's perfect for bow cuts." I leaned against the wall, trying to disguise my feelings of superiority.

"Gee, that sounds amazing. Could I try it sometime?"

I drew the paddle close to my body. "Ah," I hesitated. "You could, of course, but it's intended as a bow paddle, and I thought you might like the stern." My hand grazed over the smooth finish.

"Oh, that would be wonderful. I love paddling in the stern." Paige tuned to face the group. "Hey, the others have gathered. We'd better run." We took off like a shot, arriving breathless as Daisy called everyone together.

"Attention, girls." Daisy clapped her hands. She beckoned everyone closer. "The plan for today is to paddle over to the outpost camp with all your luggage and get set up. Looks like everyone has found a partner. Let me take attendance and jot down your teams. Please say your names and something about yourselves when I point to you." She pointed to a pair. "You first."

"Madge is my name, and I paddle with my family all the time." She waved her hand at the girl standing next to her. "This is my neighbour, Darlene."

Darlene giggled. "I guess you know my name now?" She crossed her eyes at Madge. "I live two houses away from Madge, and we're best friends." They linked arms.

Daisy pointed to another pair.

"I'm Jane, and I've paddled a little, but the fact is, my mother sent me to the outpost camp to get me moving." She bent her head, cheeks turning pink. Jane was a short, chubby girl with a round, dimpled face.

"Me too, Jane. My mom said I needed to do something other than read this summer." Jane's partner smiled as she pushed her glasses up her nose. "My name is Laura."

A very tall girl spoke up next. "My name is Courtney, and I love anything that can be done outdoors." She appeared quite fit and athletic. Her partner was a midget in comparison. Small and petite in every way described Dora the best.

Daisy selected another pair.

"I'm Randi, and this is my cousin Georgie. We're here for adventure and to have a chance to hang out together."

"Yes," agreed Georgie. They hugged one another. "We live hundreds of kilometers apart and only get to spend time together in the summer. This is such a cool way to visit," she said, eyes sparkling.

"I guess you're the last pair, Jan. We've all heard of your exploits, but who is your partner?" said Daisy.

"I'm Paige. Jan and I go to the same school, and we seem to get into similar scrapes."

We smiled at each other.

Daisy made one last checkmark on her clipboard. "My partner is Delma. We have paddled together before, haven't we, Delma?"

"Sure have, and I chose you because if I go with you, I have a better chance of coming home." Delma pointed at Daisy. "You have the map, so where it goes, I go."

Everyone laughed. The circle was filled with eager campers, ready to set out on this new adventure. Excited chatter bubbled all around. Daisy smiled as she clapped her hands.

"Each team, find your canoe. Load and launch. You all know where the outpost camp is, so head for it. I will remind you that none of your luggage is waterproof, so don't goof around too much on your way. There'll be lots of time for that later. Jan, can I have a word with you, please, before we go?"

"Sure, Daisy. Paige, why don't you choose our canoe and put your gear in? I'll be right back."

"No problem," Paige replied.

"What's up?"

"The director just told me you're here as a junior leader. I thought I was working alone." She eyed me up and down. "Apparently, I'll benefit from your expertise?" Her face filled with disdain as she considered my diminutive size. Her words froze as they landed on me.

I bristled. "Perhaps." I examined my fingernails. "My family goes canoe tripping every year—we've had many adventures. But how about you? Tell me about your experiences as an canoe tripper." I smirked, raising an eyebrow.

She glowered.

I returned a wintry smile.

"No time for that now. I have work to do." An awkward silence filled the space between us. Daisy shrugged. "Of course, this is your first time leading, since you're so young. You'd better choose a camp name."

"Actually, I already have one."

"Oh? What is it?"

"Jantastic." I lifted both eyebrows.

"Really? Well, let's see if it fits." Her smile didn't reach her eyes. "You'll notice that one canoe is going in circles. Your first assignment, *leader*, will be to straighten them out. See you at the outpost." She harrumphed and walked away.

I stiffened. Grabbing my paddle, I headed for Paige. Not a great start to the trip. She must be jealous, and no wonder. How did they ever choose her to lead a canoe trip? Ha, she needed me more than she realized.

"Careful. Those thoughts will lead you down the wrong road," said Little Voice.

I gave a little shiver, then shook off the doubt. I joined Paige. "Let's go." I climbed into the bow, supremely glad I wasn't in the stern. It would ruin my image. *Fake it till you make it* would have to be my motto.

"Head for that circling canoe." I pointed. "Ha, they're never going to reach the outpost paddling like that. It's our job to set them straight." We paddled straight to them thanks to Paige.

CHAPTER TWELVE

We caught up with the wandering canoe. The problem was evident in an instant. Madge and Darlene both wanted to paddle on the right side, and the result was circles. "Hi, girls," I said. "Perhaps you would make better progress if one of you paddles on the left side. Madge, since you're in the bow and Darlene needs to be on her strong side to steer, would you switch?"

"And who are you to be giving us orders?" said Madge. She threw down her paddle.

"Oh, sorry. Daisy forgot to tell everyone I'm the junior leader for the outpost this year. My camp name is Jantastic."

"Gee, Jan—I mean Jantastic—I didn't know that," said Paige.

"I didn't have a chance to tell you. Anyway, back to the problem."

"I'm right-handed. I can't do anything with my left," said Madge, still a tad bit belligerent. She let her left arm flop around.

I tittered as I copied her, letting my left arm go limp.

She smiled.

"Have you tried using your left? I'm right-handed, too, but I love paddling on the left side." I paddled a few strokes.

"After lots of paddling, my left arm is now stronger than my right." I flexed my left bicep.

"Hmmm, well, perhaps I could try." She picked up her paddle, switched sides, and made a few hesitant strokes. The canoe sped ahead.

"Great job, look at you go."

They beamed at me. "Race you to the outpost," Madge shouted.

We took off, gathering speed as we went. I got into the race and paddled my hardest, but we struggled to keep up. Once Madge and Darlene had settled on sides, they proved to be excellent paddlers. "Dig in, Paige, we can't let them beat us," I shouted. The outpost dock loomed ahead.

"We'd better slow down." Worry sounded in Paige's voice. She lifted her paddle.

"Don't slow down yet. We've almost caught them. Just a few more strokes and we'll do it."

Shrugging, Paige dug in for one final effort. We surged ahead, laughing triumphantly. "Uh-oh. Duck, Paige." I bent flat in the canoe as it glided under the dock, crashing to a sudden stop against the shoreline. We both catapulted forward, leaning to the left side. The canoe tipped. We flopped out—landing with a huge splash.

Daisy waited on the shore, a smirk on her face. We dragged our canoe and soggy contents out from under the dock. Everyone was falling over with laughter. "Thanks for the icebreaker, Jantastic. Now the girls know how *not* to land a canoe." She walked away, laughing. "Get your tents set up and stuff put away."

"Hey, girls, that was a fantastic landing," said Georgie. Grinning at Randi, she added, "I wish we'd thought of that. Think of how much fun we would've had telling the folks back home."

"Yeah, you've shown us how to have fun. We'll try to beat that entrance tomorrow." They jumped into the water, whooping, then assisted us in getting our stuff on shore. That kindness sure lifted my spirits. But my face still burned.

Paige smiled and shrugged. "We won the race, and our brothers weren't here to witness our triumphant arrival. That's got to be worth something, right? Plus, we achieved our goal."

"What goal?" I mumbled.

"We got Madge and Darlene paddling together. If you hadn't intervened, they might still be paddling in circles. Good job. Now let's go set up our tent and wring out our clothes." Arm in arm, we walked away.

Randi and Georgie tittered as they linked arms with us. We headed off to get the tents set up.

CHAPTER THIRTEEN

Dear Diary,

Well, I'm at the outpost camp, and I made a real splash today. No, I don't mean I did well, but once again I made a fool of myself by crashing my canoe into the shore and tipping over. You know, it's kind of funny the result was just like last time. It got everyone laughing and joking. They were still giggling all afternoon because of it. So, I guess being an icebreaker is a sign of good leadership? Seriously, though, I'll have to think of another way to lead, or I'll run out of dry clothes. On the positive side, I met a few kindred spirits—ones I can be myself with. Sadly, Daisy is not one of them. Tomorrow, I'll have to win her favor by proving how skilled I am. That should be no problem.

Good night, Diary.

"Good morning, girls. Time to get up." Daisy blew her little whistle. Groans floated from every tent. She came into the clearing and jerked to a halt when she spotted me and Paige. Anger flitted across her face as she marched over. "What are you doing up?"

"Paige and I are early risers, so we thought we'd surprise everyone with breakfast. Sorry if we disturbed you."

"You didn't. I set an alarm, so I would be up on time. I didn't hear your alarm." She poked a stick in the fire, sending ashes everywhere, including onto breakfast.

I yanked the frying pan away. "Sorry we spoiled your plans. We were trying to be helpful." Winking at Paige, I put the pan back on the fire to keep warm. "This is ready. Shall I call the girls?"

"I'll do it." She stomped away, blowing her whistle. The girls ran over, bubbling about the first night. They lined up with their plates while Paige dished out the food.

"Yum, this is delicious," said Madge. "Sleeping outdoors always makes me hungry." A chorus of 'me too' sounded around the fire.

"So, what's up for today, Daisy?" asked Darlene.

"Could we do another race, especially against Paige and Jantastic? We almost won yesterday," said Madge.

"We did win, Madge," said Darlene. "We didn't make a splash, but neither did we crash into the shore and spill. Ha, ha." Everyone joined in the laughter, including us.

"You have to admit, it was an exciting end to the race," I added, winking at Paige. Turning to Daisy, I said, "What do you have planned for today? May I help in any way?" I was trying hard to start this day over again.

Daisy relaxed as we all glanced at her. "We have a pretty packed schedule today. First and foremost, we need to get paddling. Some of us already know how to go in circles, while others know how to stop quickly." She snickered. "Then I want to teach portaging, some basic campsite procedures, map reading, and whitewater strokes. We have two days to tune up our skills, then Wednesday morning we'll head to North Bay to our starting point at Restoule Bay, in the French River Provincial Park."

"Do we have time to learn everything we need to know for this trip?" asked Dora. She fidgeted with her utensils.

"Of course," said Daisy. "I planned it all."

"I think it sounds great, don't you, Georgie?" said Randi. "Do you remember at the last family reunion? Our moms were talking about canoe trips they had done at camp when they were young."

"Ya, I marveled that my mom was ever that young and adventurous." Georgie nudged Randi.

"Mom said she ran the French River on one of her trips and she had a life-changing incident going down some chute. Do you remember the details, Georgie?"

"Oh yes, it sounded wildly exciting. It's been the biggest family story for years. As my mom tells it, your mom and her partner, Jane, were the first pair to go down Blue Chute. They described it as a fast-flowing, large chute that cascaded over and around some gigantic guard rocks, flowing around a sharp bend, and ending up tumbling into a small widening at the bottom."

"Wh ... wh ... what happened? No one died, did they?" whispered Dora.

"Oh no," laughed Randi, "or I wouldn't be here. This happened before I was born." All the girls giggled. Dora flushed.

"Well, what did happen to make this event so life-changing?" asked Courtney.

"I think surviving was what changed their lives." Randi's whisper was solemn.

"Mom said the campers had walked along the portage to look at the chute and choose a path. The leaders told them the most important part was to line up with the opening V correctly. Then let the force of the water carry you through the chute to the end, like a wild ride at the fair. It sounded simple, so everyone expected it to go as planned. But what the leaders failed to tell them was the risk of not gliding with the current, and I guess that's what triggered the near-death experience," said Georgie.

"My mom said this brush with disaster reminded her death could come at any time. She realized she wasn't ready to meet it," said Randi.

"How so?" asked Courtney.

"Mom grew up in a Christian household, and her parents taught her from a young age about Jesus. She knew all the stories, went to church every Sunday, went to camp every summer, and played the role of Christian like a champ," said Randi.

"What do you mean, 'played the role'?" asked Dora.

"She had never accepted Jesus into her heart as savior—not until that event." A hush settled around the circle. Sticks poked into the fire, and sparks flew, but no one noticed.

Randi broke the silence. "But she didn't die, and she did accept Jesus. This is a good news story, girls." Randi jumped to her feet, lifting her hands in the air. Others joined her, but not all.

"Well, I want to know what happened—you haven't told us that part yet—get on with the story," grumbled Madge. She poked at the fire, slumped over and moody.

"Right, well they paddled upstream a little way to give themselves a chance to line up at the chute. Things appeared perfect, so they paddled down the V a little too enthusiastically, missing the exact center. This caused them to glance off one of the guard rocks, which caused them to slide off course, where they bumped hard into another guard rock, which turned their canoe sideways. That was how they ended up going down the chute—sideways," said Georgie. She glanced around expectantly.

Gasps and 'Oh, nos' filled the air.

Randi continued. "Oh, now I remember the rest. The current carried them sideways, careening off rocks, like a billiard ball on a pool table. Finally, they wedged sideways across the river at the bend, before the main chute plunged into the pool at the end. There they stayed—stuck. The water was too deep to get out, and the surge of the rapids crashed against the side of the canoe so hard that they thought it would break in two. But it remained whole and stuck. They sat there, frozen and terrified, not knowing what to do."

"Is that when your mom accepted Jesus?" asked Dora.

"It sure was! Right there in the middle of a rushing torrent, Mom and Jane prayed."

Everyone leaned forward. "What happened?" Courtney whispered.

"Mom says the hand of God pushed the bow of the canoe off the rock."

Shock and disbelief registered on faces.

"Like a literal hand?" scoffed Madge, with one eyebrow raised. An edge in her voice cut the air. I looked over, surprised.

Georgie laughed and grinned at Randi. "We don't think so, but our moms have never told us," said Georgie.

"I think my mom really believes it was God's hand—not sure if anyone else does. At any rate, the bow of the canoe popped off the rock, pointing downstream, and the canoe ran down the chute to the end," said Randi.

"A miracle or a coincidence—only God knows," I said, "but I vote for miracle. Great story, girls. Now, are you ready to tackle our adventure?"

Doubt, confidence, and fear flitted across faces. I glanced over at Daisy and was surprised at what I saw. Exasperation fairly shouted from her face, sending daggers through my heart. She hated me—but why?

CHAPTER FOURTEEN

"Now I'm more worried than ever," said Dora. "I've paddled only a little and have never run rapids—I'm gonna die, I just know it." Many heads nodded around the circle.

"Don't be ridiculous, Dora, no one's going to die," said Daisy. Her mouth set in a firm line.

Dora looked down, and I thought I saw a few tears fall.

I jumped up. "Hey, everyone, we'll all be fine. We're not going down Blue Chute. We are only going to tackle Little Pine Rapids at the beginning of the South Channel. Isn't that right, Daisy?"

"Well, since you've let the cat out of the bag, I suppose I should explain what we're doing on this trip. I had planned to save this until later." With a frustrated sigh, she said, "The plan is to paddle the upper French River from Restoule Bay West to the opening of the South Channel of the French River. You see, the French River cuts around a large island called Eighteen Mile Island, so there are two channels to the French River at this point, the North and the South. The South is a more popular canoe route because of the challenging rapids on it. It's my plan to paddle to the mouth of the South Channel the first day and camp there. Then we'll spend the next couple of days practicing our new whitewater and portaging skills on the first set of rapids—Little Pine Rapids. So, there is nothing to be afraid of—is there?" Daisy searched the faces around her and frowned.

"Daisy and I are going to teach you skills that will enable you to paddle better and run rapids, aren't we, Daisy?"

"I've already told them that." She scowled.

I looked around. The girls didn't appear convinced. "Hey, girls, they selected you for this camp because you know how to paddle. We're confident that once you've polished those skills, and we teach you some whitewater strokes, you'll ace these rapids." Heads nodded, and smiles appeared. "You've all carried canoes before, I'm sure of it. Daisy is going to show you an easy way to do it on a narrow trail, because once we've shot the rapids, we have to portage back to the top to do it again." I grinned. Excitement began to bubble, and the girls leaned towards one another to chatter. I glanced at Daisy. She gave me a grudging thumbs-up.

"Okay, then after breakfast and cleanup, we'll paddle." She handed me a piece of paper. "That's the lesson plan, Jantastic. Would you lead that session while I prepare for portaging?"

"Sure will," I said. I twirled. "I'll even try leading from inside the canoe." I flashed her a grin and twirled again.

"So childish," she said, with a half-smile on her face. She walked away.

Shrugging, I called the girls over. "We're going to practice basic paddling this morning. Paddling exactly where you want to go, no deviations." I flashed a cheeky grin at Madge. "Try to paddle from our dock to the point across the lake, then back again. Once you've mastered that, we'll paddle as a group around the perimeter of the lake to build stamina and, lastly, we'll have a little regatta. We'll even have a race that will end with everyone jumping out of their canoe, but this time, intentionally." I smiled. Excited chatter filled the air.

"That was better—less boasting, more kindness," said Little Voice.

Daisy clapped her hands. "Ok everyone, get into your canoes and raft up just offshore."

Chattering, the girls headed for the canoes. After much scraping and banging, the canoes floated together. Each canoe joined onto the one beside it with the girls holding hands. "Girls, this is a useful way to keep together when we stop for lunch on the canoe trip. It's called 'rafting'." I wet my finger and put it in the air. "Perfect."

"What's perfect, Jantastic?" asked Paige.

"The wind—it's strong enough to blow us across the lake. Hey, girls, I have a little change of plan. Does anyone have a big towel with them?"

Two girls help up very large blanket towels.

"May I borrow these? I'm going to show you a little trick."

Puzzled faces stared at me. The girls passed me their towels. I also had the girls take the painters off two canoes. I laid the towels down across two canoes and attached a paddle to each side of the towels using the painters. "Okay, girls in the center canoes, each hold up your towel sails. Now everyone hold on tight." When we lifted the sails, the rafted canoes surged forward across the lake. "Stern paddlers on the outside canoes are in charge of steering. Aim for the far shore." Giggles and gasps erupted as our combined vessel sailed across the lake, effortlessly.

"Jantastic, now this is what I call a great canoe trip," said Jane. "All I need is my blanket and book." She lay back against the stern, with a happy sigh. “To think, my mom thought I’d be working off a few pounds.” Everyone laughed.

“I did bring my book,” added Laura. She hauled a book from underneath her lifejacket. “I was hoping I would have a chance to finish—I’m just at the climax.” Amazement filled many faces.

“Well, ah, Laura, I think you’d better stick that in a waterproof bag and tuck it away. Remember, our paddling will end today with everyone jumping overboard and learning to swim with our canoes.”

“Oops, I forgot.” A rosy glow appeared on her face.

I gave her a friendly nudge. “No problem, I have a dry sack here that should keep your book safe today. Perhaps you would read us a part of the story tonight?”

“Oh, I’d love to.” Laura handed the book over to me.

“Okay, everyone. Our little break is over. We’ve reached the opposite shore. Please undo the sails and get ready to practice paddling. Paige and I will follow behind to offer hints and help where needed. Then off you go to the point across the lake,” I said, pointing to the destination. “Wait for everyone else there.” I had picked a different point to paddle to, since our sailing expedition had taken us to the original point. I shrugged. “Oh well, even good plans have to change sometimes.”

The canoes split up and shot off, splashing and bumping as they went. I grinned—humor restored. I glanced back across the water to the outpost camp. A lone figure stood on the dock, hands on hips.

CHAPTER FIFTEEN

Clearly, improvisation was not allowed. Daisy waited at the end of the dock, hands still on hips, when we arrived once again at the outpost camp. I put on my cheery face and said, "Hi, Daisy. Have you come to watch our little contest?"

"You're late."

"Oh, I didn't know there was a scheduled time to complete this lesson. Sorry." I shrugged. "Would you like me to call off the contest?" The girls waited, holding their breath, for the signal to start the event.

Daisy gazed out at them, then shook her head and walked away. I blew out the breath I'd been holding. I turned to the girls, trying to smile.

"Okay, does everyone understand the rules?" Four canoes lined up in front of me. "Darlene, will you explain the contest again, please?"

Darlene blushed. "First, we'll turn our canoes around and back up until our sterns touch the dock. When everyone is in position, Jantastic will blow the whistle, and we'll race to First Island, jump out at the beach and switch spots, so the bow paddler is in the stern and the stern paddler is in the bow, then we'll paddle back and touch the dock. Once we touch the dock, we have to jump out of the canoe and swim with it to the outpost swimming rock. Climb in again—in deep water—then paddle back to the outpost. The first canoe back wins a treat at the Tuck Shop. Is that right?"

"Perfect. Any questions? Is everybody ready? Okay, one, two, three." The whistle trilled.

The canoes took off—everyone striving to be the first canoe away, but no one tipped. They were pretty evenly matched on the way to First Island. Paige and I followed behind the paddlers. Surprisingly, Laura and Jane were in the lead, and Georgie and Randi followed close behind.

"Well, it appears the bookworms can also paddle when they want to," I said, pointing.

"Yes, but look, Jantastic," said Paige.

Dora was standing up to change places—then kerplunk, she landed in the water. The canoe tipped. Out plopped Courtney.

"Need any help?" I croaked, barking out a short laugh.

Water cascaded off both. They waved, then emptied their canoe. Sloshing through the water, they changed places and began to paddle. They paddled in circles.

"Take a gander at that canoe, Paige. They're mismatched." The bow was deep in the water.

"You nailed it, Jantastic. That must be the problem." Courtney was huge, and Dora was small.

"Something's wrong, Jantastic," yelled Courtney. "We're both paddling as hard as we can, but going in circles. I can't understand it—we did okay before." She dropped her paddle.

"Sorry, Courtney, I'm trying, really I am, but this thing just won't turn." Dora threw her paddle down. The canoe floated aimlessly.

"Switch back again, girls," I yelled. Shrugging, they changed places. They paddled straight.

"Wow, we can paddle again." An amazed smile blazed on their faces. They dug in and zoomed ahead, calling out a challenge to catch them.

"Oh, Jantastic, look over at the dock," called Paige.

"Now, what?" I mumbled. Two canoes had overturned. Laura and Jane's canoe, and Georgie and Randi's had turned turtle. "They must have jumped out of their canoes at the same time, on the same side."

"It seems like they've all decided to swim to the rock without righting the canoe—big mistake, right, Jantastic?"

"That would be my opinion. Canoes are hard to push like that."

"Oh wow, Madge and Darlene are darting to the lead. They're at the dock and are jumping out," said Paige. Her hands clapped over her mouth. Their canoe tipped as well.

"Oops, that leaves Courtney and Dora. Look, they've caught up. They've jumped out—their canoe remained upright." Paige clapped her hands.

"Go, girls." I threw my hands in the air. "Do you think they can get back into the canoe?"

"They've had practice," said Paige. Laughter spilled out of her. "Not sure if they can manage this. Dora has such a size disadvantage."

"Oh, but Courtney knows that already and is lifting Dora up so she can grab the gunnel. Wow, Dora's in the canoe and is leaning over to help Courtney." We both held our breath as we watched.

"They did it." We high-fived each other. I wanted to twirl so badly but thought better of it. Twirling and canoes probably didn't mix. "Let's paddle back to meet them at the dock." By the time we got there, they were already on shore, beaming.

Soaked, excited girls dragged their canoes on shore to empty them. We all pitched in to help.

"Did you have fun?" I yelled. Cheers greeted me. Time for lunch, and everyone was ready for it. Daisy smiled from the campfire. She had prepared lunch. I smiled back—did this mean peace?

"Eat hearty, girls, because after lunch, we'll be portaging," said Daisy. Campers flopped to the ground. "I'm not trying to torture you. Remember, on this canoe trip we'll have to portage, and it is much easier if it's done the right way. We're going to shoot a set of rapids multiple times, so we have to bring our canoes back to the top of the rapids after we run them, in order to shoot them again. If you can't portage, then you can't run the rapids."

Heads nodded.

"Do we have to solo portage?" asked Dora. She wrung her hands.

"No, you may choose to double portage, but the path is narrow and zig-zags, I've been told," said Daisy. "Okay, girls, get your dishes cleaned up and bring your canoes to the flat area above the outpost camp." Their eyes immediately swiveled to the steep path ascending to the flats. "Carry the canoes up there?" said a chorus of whining voices.

"Yep, that's your introduction to portaging."

Groans filled the air, followed by lots of murmuring of I can't, I won't, not possible, and one small voice asking if she could call her Mom. Daisy put her finger to her mouth and waited for quiet.

"Since Jantastic has portaged before, perhaps she can give us some pointers?" Daisy sent a challenging glint in my direction.

I shrugged. "No problem, Daisy. As a rule, I choose to portage the canoe rather than the packs." The girls exchanged skeptical expressions around the campfire.

"Really, Jantastic? You're not just saying that to get us to do it?" asked Darlene.

"Of course not, and here's why. The canoe weighs between sixty and eighty pounds, but so do most full packs, and the food pack can weigh a hundred pounds on a long trip. Plus, canoe packs are big and lumpy. There's always something sticking into your back as you carry it. However, the canoe has a comfortable yoke that fits around your neck and spreads equal weight onto both shoulders. Nothing jabs you. It's well balanced, so at times I only have to support it with one arm while resting the other. When I get tired and need a rest, all I have to do is find a tree with a low branch. I walk my canoe into that tree until the bow rests on the branch, then I get out from under it and stretch my shoulders." Heads nodded.

"But I don't understand why we can't double portage?" said Laura.

"Have any of you ever dressed up as a donkey or camel for Halloween or Christmas?"

Puzzlement appeared on faces. "I was a camel in a Christmas play, once. I was the rear, and my friend Lucy was the head," said Jane.

"What was it like being the rump? Was it hard to follow Lucy?" I asked.

"Impossible." Jane threw her hands in the air. "I couldn't see a thing, and I kept tripping. I was told we were pretty funny." Everyone laughed.

"Picture being in the rear of the canoe as you portage. All you can see is the rump of your partner. Your job is to follow her exactly, and if you don't, you crash into trees, trip over rocks, or fall over ledges. It's as impossible as being the tail of a camel."

Giggles filled the air.

"But I'm too small to carry a canoe," moaned Dora.

"Stand up, Dora." She did. I stood beside her. "Who's the tallest girl?"

"You are, but just barely," they shouted. Dora blushed. I squeezed her shoulder. "It's not about size. It's about technique and determination. We'll help you with both, right, Daisy?"

Daisy frowned.

Good grief, what did I do this time? I jumped to my feet and shuffled off to find my canoe.

"Okay, girls, let's begin by carrying our canoes in pairs, up that hill," said Daisy.

The girls struggled up the hill with their canoes—then flaked out at the top, chests heaving. I motored up the hill solo portaging.

"How did you manage that, Jantastic? You're not even breathing hard," puffed Madge.

"Practice, I guess. I've portaged dozens of times in my life. It's not that hard once you master the technique." I lowered my canoe with a gentle thump to the ground—then stared at Daisy, eyebrow raised.

The campers followed my gaze and also looked at Daisy, who was leaning against a tree, arms crossed.

"Thanks for the demo, Jantastic." She didn't sound thankful. "Now, I will teach the technique. Listen up, everyone, let's begin."

The lesson lasted an hour and was followed by two hours of practice. When it ended, exhausted girls stumbled or rolled down the hill to the campsite. No chatter, no excitement, just fatigue. Daisy brought up the rear.

Despondency draped heavily on the girls' shoulders. Something needed to be done to restore their enthusiasm. I glanced at Daisy. She sat on a log, head in hands. Hmm, no help there. Then I had an idea. "Anyone want a swim?" I asked. Instantly, the campers revived and dashed off to get suits on.

The swim lifted spirits. They compared biceps in the water. A babbling, slightly boastful bunch gathered around the fire for dinner. They bragged about what husky trippers they were and marvelled at my apparent ease in portaging. Daisy was strangely quiet.

CHAPTER SIXTEEN

After dinner, I moseyed over to speak with Daisy. "Hi. This seems like a pretty keen group of girls. Your paddling lesson hit the spot, don't you think?" Silence. "They caught on to the portaging pretty well." Silence. I started to walk away.

"I'm the leader of this outpost, right?"

Puzzled, I stared at her. "Sure, you are."

"Then why don't I feel like it?"

I shrugged.

"You've taken over."

"What?" I jerked. Thoughts whirled through my head.

Little Voice spoke. *"Jan, just reassure her. Be kind, caring and encouraging."*

"No, I haven't. You asked for help. You got it. I'm not sure how that's 'taking over.'" I stomped off. Why should I even try? Clearly, she wasn't. Could I help it if I knew more than she did? I dove into my tent to think. I wasn't there very long before Paige peeked in.

"Are you okay?" she asked. "I saw you storm away from Daisy. She's gone for a walk, and you're hiding in our tent. We're all sitting around the campfire, waiting." She plopped down beside me to give me a quick hug. "Hey, girl, you've done a great job today. Don't blow it now. Come on out and sing with us or something. Smooth it over, so Daisy can ease on in when she's ready. Remember, you told me God called you for this job. If that's the case, then he must have also equipped you. I don't know much about this stuff, but if God is as important to you as you've led me to believe, then shouldn't you be showing it?" She rose to her feet and stepped past the flap. "I'll tell everyone that 'Mighty Mouse'—that's your nickname by the way—was so tired from portaging that she had to take a nap." Giggling, she ran to join the others.

"Listen to Paige. I'm working on her. I sent her along as an encourager to help you to do your job," said Little Voice.

I sat bolt upright. Little Voice's words rang loud and clear. How could I have forgotten I was here to do a job, and he had it all planned out? How did I ever let those negative thoughts in? I left the tent. No sign of Daisy. "Lord, what should I do? If I start anything, she'll accuse me of taking over again."

"Paige told you to sing, so sing," said Little Voice.

"I hear you have a new name for me," I called. The girls ducked their heads. "Mighty Mouse happens to be one of my favourite cartoons. Thanks." I laughed and joined the circle. "Let's sing. Who knows some camp songs?" Hands flew into the air.

Dora called, "This Little Light of Mine."

"Great song—This little light of mine, I'm gonna let it shine ..." That was just the beginning. We sang and sang. Clearly campfire singing was a favorite activity. We'd just finished the fifth song when Daisy arrived with a smile on her face.

"The beautiful singing just called to me," she said. "I brought back marshmallows, chocolate, and graham crackers. Does anyone know what that combination makes?"

"S'mores," everyone yelled. "Yippee." The girls dashed around to find sticks and started roasting marshmallows.

"After our snack, we'll have a devotional time. Hey, Jan, can I speak with you for a moment while the girls are making their snack?"

"Sure." We went for a walk up the hill, neither saying anything. I hunched my shoulders, keeping my focus on the path.

Daisy took an audible breath. "Jan, I owe you an apology. I'm sorry for my accusations. You were right. I asked for help, and you gave it. I let the green monster of envy get a hold of my thoughts, instead of being thankful for the great helper the director arranged." Her breath escaped on a slow sigh.

"Well, you're not the only one who has to apologize. The Spirit clearly reminded me to be an encourager to you, but I let anger get in the way. I should understand where you're coming from. I'm the youngest in my family, and my brainy sister and know-it-all brother always remind me they know more than me. The trouble is they do, but that doesn't make it any easier to accept." I grinned. "Can we do this together?" I twirled.

"You bet. The Lord put us together for a reason. From this point on, let's trust him. Actually, trusting God is the theme of our devotions. A coincidence, do you think?" said Daisy. "By the way, what's with the twirling?"

"Just my immature inner self bubbling out." I grinned, linking arms with her.

"I forget you are just out of the nursery sometimes." She nudged me in the ribs, smiling.

"Let's go back. I'm missing my s'more."

"From now on, we'll be partners," said Daisy.

I regarded her. Perhaps this would work out, but we'd been upset with each other for two days. Was the relationship really mended?

CHAPTER SEVENTEEN

"Girls, we're going to start a study on trusting God. Who can tell me what trust means?" Daisy peered at all the faces. Courtney put up her hand.

"I think trust means that no matter what happens, you have to believe God has got your back."

"Does that include when bad things happen?" asked Daisy.

"I think it must, because when everything is going well, it's easy to trust," added Darlene.

"Okay, here's another question. Is it God's job to always do what we want?"

"No," everyone called at once.

"Why not?"

Darlene's hand flew into the air. "Because God is God. He's the boss. He's in control and he calls the shots, not us."

"Well, if that's the case, how can I trust him?" Daisy asked.

The girls glanced at each other. The hard question stumped them.

A little voice called from the back of the circle. "Because we know God loves us. After all, he sent Jesus to save us, even though we were bad." Laura was the youngest camper and avoided notice. Everyone nodded.

"Good answer, Laura. Now let's see what the Bible says. I want you to memorize these two verses this week. Jantastic, will you pass around the memory cards, please?"

I leapt up and did this.

"Verse one—Proverbs 3:5-6—Trust in the Lord with all your heart and lean not on your own understanding. In all your ways, acknowledge him and he shall direct your path.

"Verse two—Philippians 4:6-7—Be anxious for nothing, but in everything by prayer and supplication with thanksgiving, let your requests be made known to God. And the peace of God, which surpasses all understanding, will guard your hearts and minds, through Christ Jesus.

"Girls, I think this trip will challenge you in many ways. These two verses will help you deal with situations over which you have no control. Read them, think about them, and memorize them so that when trouble comes, you are armed and ready. Before closing tonight, I wonder if you would share a canoe trip adventure with the girls, Jantastic—oh Mighty Mouse?" The girls giggled. "But before you start, tell me, do you think God actively helped you on your adventure?"

"Absolutely, Daisy, though it took us a while to figure that out. Some of us are slow learners ..." I pointed to myself and grinned. "... but I've found that God is patient. My sister, brother, and I went on a kids-only canoe trip a couple of summers ago. Each of us had something to prove to ourselves and our parents. The summer prior to this trip, my family had done part of the same trip. That's where I discovered I was a coward."

The girls gasped. Astounded eyes stared at me.

"During the trip we had to run one small chute. Now, I know it wasn't very big, but in my mind, I had built that chute up to be an impossible obstacle, so when it came time to shoot it, I panicked. I threw down my paddle and covered my eyes."

I looked at the girls. Laughing faces filled the circle, while giggles filled the air.

"I knew I had to conquer that obstacle or it would haunt me all my life. So, I proposed the kids-only canoe trip to face this threat again. My brother, Brad, wanted to prove he was old enough to go adventuring on his own—at the time, he was fourteen years old—and my older sister, Susie, wanted to prove there was nothing she couldn't think her way through. So, all of us had different reasons for wanting to go, but each of us excluded God."

"Jantastic, what do you mean by 'you excluded God?' We can't exclude him because he's always there, isn't he?" asked Dora.

"Yes, that's true, but we didn't consult him about any of our plans. We tried to meet the challenges of that trip in our own power and strength. God used that adventure to make his presence known to us."

"Weren't you a Christian when you made that trip, like my mom?" asked Randi.

"I was a Christian, and so were my siblings, but our understanding of God and our faith wasn't very good. Brad had begun to believe God didn't exist. He felt he was completely in charge of his own life."

"Where did you go on this trip?" asked Courtney.

"We paddled down the Sauble River from East Bull Lake to Cameron Falls, but we didn't manage to paddle to Cameron Falls."

"Why didn't you?"

"We lost our canoe before we got there."

Gasps sounded around the circle.

"God knew we needed to be shaken out of our self-reliance to become God-reliant. So, he allowed this little accident to wake us up."

"What happened?" several girls chimed together.

"We paddled over a waterfall. Our canoe got smashed on the way down, and all our provisions floated downstream with the broken canoe. The incident stranded us a long way from our destination with Susie injured, no food, no sleeping bags, and no clothes. But God provided."

The girls gasped. "What did God provide and how did he do it?"

"Well, that's too long a story for tonight, but I will summarize the basics. God provided fish every day we were out there and a method to start a fire and cook them. He provided the means to make a raft and a shelter. He gave my sister a photographic memory, and she told us where we were most of the time. And he protected us from a wounded bear that followed us. I'm here today because God rescued me, and I'm no longer afraid, because now I know I can take my fears to him. Just like our memory verse says." I squeezed my eyes shut, remembering the adventure.

Daisy and Paige stared at me with wide eyes.

Daisy snapped out of her trance. "Okay, girls. Time to brush our teeth and hit the sack. Let's pray before you go."

We bowed our heads, and Daisy prayed. "Amen."

The silence erupted into excited chatter as the girls scurried to get ready for bed.

I overheard lots of discussion about my trip along with excited conjecture about how it might have happened.

Daisy and I sat by the fire, gazing into its embers. "I'm exhausted, and we have another full day tomorrow," murmured Daisy.

"What's on the schedule?"

"More paddling, of course, but we'll add on bow cuts and stern draws to equip the girls for whitewater, then map reading and compasses. After dinner, we have to paddle the canoes back to main camp so they can be loaded on the trailer, and we'll spend an hour packing all the kitchen gear and nonperishables into packs. We'll hike back to the outpost with the empty knapsacks for our tents and sleeping bags—then pack those in the morning."

"Wow, that *is* a full day. We'll be too tired to listen to devotionals."

Daisy grinned. "I think not. Well, goodnight."

"Now, that's the way to get along, mutual respect and kindness. Good job," said Little Voice.

I couldn't have agreed more. I sure hoped it would last.

CHAPTER EIGHTEEN

Dear Diary,

The outpost has been a very busy place. Yesterday, we paddled and portaged—today we paddled and had an orienteering race, as a way of teaching navigation. The girls caught on well. I wonder if Daisy is really as terrific a navigator as she seems. Has she done it for real on a wilderness trip or just in orienteering competitions, like we had today? Oh well, it's not a skill I have. On our trips, Brad or Dad always navigated.

Man, am I tired. At the end of this very busy day, we had to paddle our canoes back to camp, then pack everything except perishable foods, our tents, and sleeping bags. There sure were lots of packs already. I wonder if Daisy plans to count them before we go?

I yawned.

Got to go, diary. Talk to you later.

"Wow, Paige is asleep already—smart girl." I switched off my light and then snuggled into my sleeping bag.

It seemed like only minutes later when I rolled over and peeked out of the tent to find the sun smiling at me. Yikes, I had overslept. I nudged Paige. "I think we slept in—best get moving. We have to stuff our sleeping bags and roll the tent this morning."

"Relax, Jantastic, I don't hear anyone else."

I sat still and listened. She was right. I poked my nose out of the tent and, sure enough, the whole camp was quiet. "Do you have a watch, Paige?"

"Wait a minute, I'll dig it out of my pack. Ah, here it is. Wow, it's late. It's eight a.m. Better get moving if we want to be on the road by ten." We set to work. Once I'd stuffed my sleeping bag and dressed, I dove out of the tent to wake the others. "Oh, rise and shine, campers," I sang.

Groans and thrown pillows greeted my song. It seemed we weren't the only ones who were tired. Suddenly, the aroma of bacon tickled my nose. I followed the smell and found Daisy busy with the task of cooking breakfast. "Wow, Daisy, I didn't hear a thing. Thanks for making breakfast, but why didn't you wake me?"

Daisy smiled as she flipped a pancake. "I can't have you doing all the work, now can I, or that green monster will rear its awful head again." She laughed, whistling a merry tune. I smiled and visited each tent to get campers moving.

"It appears we have everything packed, Daisy." I made a final sweep of the outpost. I gave the thumbs-up.

"Okay, girls, let's hike out to the main camp and start our adventure," directed Daisy. Everybody whooped, excited to get started. "When we get to camp, load your packs and paddles into the van, then climb in." Minutes later, we were on our way.

I climbed in with the rest of the girls, then watched Daisy as she chatted with the driver. She joined us. "Relax, everyone. It will take about three hours to reach our starting point," she said. Everyone chattered for a while, then silence reigned, as one by one the girls fell asleep.

Daisy clapped her hands. "We're here, girls. I just saw the sign."

Sleeping beauties yawned and stretched.

"Now, remember to get your stuff out of the van and pile it by the launching area. Please don't spread it around, or we may forget something. Then come back and help unload the other packs and canoes," said Daisy. The van stopped, and the girls poured out—wide awake—bouncing with excitement.

Paige took our tent pack and went to help with the canoes. Once everything was unloaded, I made a final check in the van. It was empty, which was good. But I sensed something was wrong. What was it? I counted the canoes. Yep, there were six, enough for two girls per canoe. Then I counted the packs. One kitchen pack, one equipment pack and five tent/sleeping bag packs. "Five tent packs, but we have six groups." The van was taking off—I ran to flag it down. A curious face peered out of the window. "Sorry, guys, may I take one more gander in the van, please?"

"Sure, Jantastic, but I don't think you'll find anything."

I checked anyway. The van was empty. I took a look inside the canoe trailer. It too was empty. "Thanks, fellas." I hung my head. *"Now what do I do, Lord?"*

Daisy came over. "Is there a problem?"

"Yep, there is. I think we left one pack behind."

She jumped back, panic-stricken, face white as paste.

"I seem to remember seeing a pack by the lodge with a paddle leaning on it." Girls were milling all around, so I presumed it had been loaded with the other bags.

I could tell Daisy was irritated, but she said nothing. I tried to remain calm. "Why don't we have the girls locate their packs and paddles and stand beside them, that way we'll find out who is missing something. What do you think?"

"It doesn't matter what I think, now does it? We're in a mess no matter what we do." She stomped off to tell the girls to claim their gear.

She blamed me. The nerve. I wasn't in charge of loading. Everyone loaded their own stuff. I glared at Daisy, fuming.

"Trust me, I've got this," said Little Voice.

But I was mad, so I wasn't listening.

From across the driveway, I heard wailing, and I knew who had forgotten their bag—Madge and Darlene. I went over to help.

"Jantastic, somehow we left one of our bags behind," moaned Darlene.

"Do you know what was in it?" I asked.

"It was the tent bag. It had our tent and Dora's and Courtney's tent." Darlene slumped like mush to the ground.

"Why did you have two tents in your bag, and where are your sleeping bags?" I asked.

"Dora had a much larger knapsack than we had—enough room for all the sleeping bags—and we were able to squeeze the two tents into our smaller bag. We were so proud of ourselves for working out a solution without help, weren't we, girls?" They all nodded, sending imploring gazes my way. Hmm, perhaps if I snapped my fingers the sack would appear? Like I could do anything.

"You can't, but I can. Trust me," said Little Voice.

Kicking a stone out of my way, I mulled over the reminder to trust God. I straightened with determination and walked over to Daisy. She was leaning against a tree, staring. Doing nothing—saying nothing. Tapping a light fingertip on her shoulder, I asked, "Maybe this has happened for a reason, Daisy. Could we gather the girls together to pray for God's help? Convert our memory verse to action?" I watched her closely. She closed her eyes and took a big breath.

"Girls, gather around, please." Everyone shuffled over. "We have a little problem. Two tents were left behind." The girls gasped. "We're going to pray for wisdom. Let's all join hands and bow our heads."

Everyone complied. Some cried.

"Lord, we have a problem that you already know about," Daisy said. "Please help us find a solution so we can see your guiding hand at work. We thank you, in Jesus's name. Amen."

CHAPTER NINETEEN

"Whoopee, the answer has just come to me," I said. I twirled in a circle.

"What's the answer, Jantastic?" Everyone stared at me.

"We have four knapsacks with one tent and two sleeping bags in each, correct?"

"Yes."

"We have one knapsack with four sleeping bags, correct?"

"Yes, Jantastic, but what are you getting at?" asked Daisy. Her hands were on her hips, and she tapped her toe.

"We have three-person tents, so we'll put three in each tent. Cozy and warm. It'll be great." I beamed. Everyone jumped up and down, then negotiated about who would tent together.

"That was neat," said Dora.

"What was?" said Daisy.

"God answered our prayer with an alternative plan. Our plan was two campers per tent. His plan was for three. Do you think he'll tell us why? This is just like the verse you had us learn."

Daisy smiled and nodded her head. The cloud hanging over her floated away. She cleared her throat.

"All right, girls, it's time to stow the gear in your canoe. Make sure you strap it in well. Put on your lifejackets and push off from shore. We'll raft together just offshore to pray."

There was a great deal of commotion as everyone sorted out their gear. Suddenly, angry voices could be heard above the general noise.

"That's my paddle. Give it back." Courtney grabbed hold of the blade of Darlene's paddle. A tug of war ensued. Voices grew louder.

"What's all the hubbub?" I asked.

"Darlene stole my paddle," accused Courtney.

"Did not." Darlene glowered at Courtney.

"Well, most of the paddles are similar. Why don't we just get another for you?" I glanced around but didn't see any spare paddles. "Does anyone have an extra paddle in their canoe?" Everyone shook their heads. A picture of a single paddle leaning on a single knapsack appeared in my mind. Oh, no, Lord, not a paddle? How would he help us with this? I cringed and then took a deep breath.

I moseyed over to Daisy. "Would you come for a little walk with me, please?"

"Right in the middle of shoving off? You've picked a fine time to cozy up for a chat." She noted my tense face and walked.

"Okay, what's up this time?" She stood with her hands on hips.

"It appears we left a paddle behind with the knapsack." I squeezed my eyes shut, tensing. I opened one. Daisy just stood there as if she were in a trance. Then she laughed.

"Daisy, are you okay?"

"Oh, yes. I'm fine. If there's one thing you can't do without on a canoe trip, it's your paddle."

"Unless you lose your canoe." We fell back, helpless with laughter.

"Have you prayed about this yet?"

"Yep, but I would love to pray with you, since we're a team. We sure need the help of our other team member." Looking up, we took our needs to God.

"Father, we need your help again," I said. "We need your wisdom to know what to do about the missing paddle. We're at the starting point of our trip. We have no vehicles and no town close by, no phone to call anyone and no one to call, except you. We give this to you. May it be a growing time for the bunch of us. Give us your peace. Amen." Relief flowed through me. "I feel better already."

"Does that mean that God has sent you a plan?"

"Not yet, but I'm sure he will. Let's walk back to the girls, and perhaps we'll know what to do when we get there."

"We'd better walk slow, then. It's not very far," Daisy said, with twinkling eyes. We linked arms—we would face this together.

CHAPTER TWENTY

I spied the girls all huddled in a glum group. Giving a wave, we beckoned them over. Curiosity was written on all their faces.

"Why are you two so chipper?" asked Darlene.

"Ya, we'll have to cancel this trip or leave a canoe behind. It's a catastrophe," grumped Madge. She glowered at Courtney.

"Ya, a paddle's been left behind, and we can't very well share," said Courtney. She glowered back.

"Well, whoever left the pack behind probably left the paddle with it," said Dora. She leveled an accusatory stare at Madge. Then chaos broke out. Tension built as the girls paired off to accuse one another of the mistake.

Lord, help us. Why did this always happen? The blame game never solved anything, but here we were, apparently stranded, standing around playing it.

I jumped onto a tree stump. Anger radiated from my face. "Stop," I yelled. Everyone stood like statues. Some with arms in the air, some with pointing fingers. "Is this the way to handle a disaster? If my siblings and I had plopped down at the bottom of the waterfall and wailed, 'not fair' to God, then spent our time blaming Brad, we would still be there." I glared. "Who can tell me what we should do?"

A meek voice spoke up. "Ask God for help and trust him to provide it?" said Laura.

"Correct." We turned to look at Daisy.

"I was waiting for a break in the action to suggest that," she said. "Girls, you know we planned none of these problems, so as we trust in a loving, heavenly Father, we have to believe this event is within his control. Why? Because he has assured us it is. Let's pray." We bowed our heads. "Father, we give this problem to you. Please help us. Amen"

Eyes opened. Some searched, as if expecting a paddle to float down from the sky. A kernel of an idea formed in my mind.

I winked—Daisy grinned. "Though God always answers prayer, the solution is not always as we would like. As you can see, no paddle has miraculously appeared."

Shoulders slumped—a few tears glistened. "God is able to do that, but I guess that's not his plan this time. What he has done is send me an idea."

Faces lit up. Daisy raised an eyebrow.

"On this type of canoe trip, we haven't planned much paddling. We have only to paddle across this widening of the French River and make camp. Then, we're going to take turns shooting the rapids."

"We know that, Jantastic, but we still need a paddle to get there and to shoot the rapids," grumbled Madge. Throwing her arms in the air, she paced. "Oh, why do bad things always happen to me?"

"Not just to you, what about the rest of us?" said Laura. Voices grew louder—faces reddened, until a small voice asked a question.

"What plan has God sent you, Jantastic?" said Jane. Hope shone from her eyes.

"We'll attach a rope to the canoe with the single paddle and have three people paddling two canoes."

The girls peered at me, then at each other. As if on command, they broke into small groups to discuss this option. Daisy gave me the thumbs-up, then looked toward the sky, mouthing, 'Thank you'.

"This could be fun," Courtney said, excitement lightening her voice.

"Yeah, I bet no one else has ever done this. Think of the stories we can tell." Georgie said.

"It will be like a train on the water, with the engine at the front," Randi added with a giggle.

"A canoe-train," said Jane, eyes twinkling. Everyone danced around, catching the vision.

I stood there, marvelling yet again that God could change a trip-ending disaster into a cause for joy. I was bursting with enthusiasm. I just had to twirl—so I did.

"Good grief, there she goes again," said Daisy. "Let's take a moment and thank God for this great way to learn about him." Excited heads bowed. We prayed.

CHAPTER TWENTY-ONE

Six canoes floated rafted together in the calm bay. We tied Dora and Courtney's canoe to Darlene and Madge's canoe by the bowline. The girls smiled, light chatter bubbling all around. Daisy held up a map, which she had been perusing.

"Here's the plan, girls." She pointed to the map. "We are at the landing of Restoule Bay, and we have to paddle straight across this bay and continue across the widening of the French River, west to the mouth of the South Channel of the French River—right here." She marked the spot with her finger. Campers who were close enough leaned forward for a peek.

I hadn't reviewed our route until this moment. Surprise fluttered in my belly. "Wow, Daisy, I didn't realize it was quite that far." I cast my eyes over our canoe train.

"Oh, it's not that far—about fourteen kilometers," quipped Daisy.

I glanced at my watch.

"We'll be a bit later getting to camp because of the slow start, but we should still make it before dark."

I looked down, biting my lip.

"Don't forget whose plan this is. God's got this," said Little Voice.

Eagerness filled me. I nodded.

Courtney leaned over, pointing at the map. "Do you see all the islands, Daisy? Will it be hard to steer around them?"

"Piece of cake if you're an experienced navigator, like me," replied Daisy. "Time to get paddling, girls." She folded the map with care and put it in a waterproof bag.

I watched her. "How will you know where to go?"

Daisy glared. "It's a straight line to our destination. We'll keep the shoreline on our left shoulder." She started paddling—discussion over.

Don't be a doubter, I thought. "Right, you are, skipper. Would you like me paddling at the rear, and you can be in the front?"

Relief shone on her face. "Yes, please, Jantastic, that would be great. Perhaps you could watch over our canoe-train?"

"Will do."

"Hey, where'd those clouds come from?" said Jane. "I hope it doesn't rain."

"Yeah, and the wind's picking up, as well," said Laura.

"Oh, stop playing weathergirl, and come sing with us," said Darlene. "My paddle's clean and bright, flashing with silver ..." The rest of the group joined in. Everyone set their canoes in motion, happiness beaming, in time to the singing.

"Oh, how I love paddling in a group, with lots of singing and camaraderie—thank you, Lord. Lead us on," I prayed.

The first hour went very well.

"Is the wind pushing us sideways?" asked Paige.

"I think so—we're being driven north by the waves," I replied.

"It's harder to paddle, as well," said Paige.

I checked around me. The canoes were much more spread out. The canoe train lagged way to the rear.

"We'd better paddle back to check on the canoe train." We turned around and paddled up beside them.

"Hey, girls, are you having trouble keeping up? Must be hard to hold your course in this wind."

Darlene sat in the stern of the rear canoe. She put down her paddle with a groan. "Any chance we could take a break, Jantastic? I think my arm is going to fall off." She grimaced.

I laughed. "I bet you're not the only one who is tired, Darlene, but you do have more cause than most."

"Hey, what about us?" shouted Courteny and Dora. "We're the engine, after all? Vroom, vroom, all power, no smoke." Giggling, they stopped paddling and grinned at the caboose.

I pointed. "I see an island with a sand beach straight ahead. I'll paddle up to Daisy and ask if we can stop for a rest—perhaps even a snack. I'm starving." Paige and I shot ahead. Soon, we landed on the island, staggering out to stretch.

"Oh, this feels wonderful," said Dora. "I never knew my shoulders could be this tired."

"My shoulders are fine, but my back is killing me," said Courtney. She was a tall girl.

Daisy pulled the daypack out of her canoe. "Snack time, come and get it."

The girls mobbed her. Laughing, she moseyed over for a chat, pulling out the map as she walked. Surveying the shoreline to the left, then ahead of her, she pointed to the map. "This is where we are."

"Oh, wow." I checked around me and then back at the page. "How can you tell if this is the island we're on and not that one?" I pointed to an island just north of where she indicated and giggled nervously.

"It's simple. You have to look at the shape of the islands." She outlined the figure on the map. "You see, it's the very same."

"Nope, I can't see—not unless I'm a bird." All I saw was a sand beach, surrounded by trees I couldn't see over.

Daisy laughed. "Well, it's good that I'm navigating, then, Jantastic." She patted my shoulder. "Okay, girls," she said. "Time to go. We're burning daylight."

"Good grief, you sound just like my brother, Brad." I laughed. "He said that right before we went over the waterfall." I glanced at Daisy and gave a nervous shrug.

CHAPTER TWENTY-TWO

We piled into the canoes and pushed off from shore. Immediately most of the canoes were pushed back on shore. "Wow, the wind has increased," I said.

Daisy stared at the waves. "And the waves have, too," she added. "Let's paddle around to the other side of this island. It will shelter us from the elements for a while."

"Great idea. Girls, dig in—paddle hard. Follow Daisy around the island." They all nodded and followed—with difficulty.

During the break, we had decided to switch up the paddlers of the canoe train, so a fresh group battled the waves now. Finally, after several anxious minutes, everyone pulled away from shore and made it to the shelter of the other side.

"Let's rest for a moment in the lee of this island," I suggested. The weary girls dropped their paddles. Paige and I paddled over to Daisy. "Do you think we could island hop so we can use the islands to block us from the waves? It shouldn't matter as long as we head west." I asked. "Will you be able to keep us on course?"

"Piece of cake," she responded. "Using the islands to block wind and waves sounds like a good idea. Let's go."

"Don't you want to go to shore to pull out the map?" I raised my eyebrows as I leaned closer, whispering, "Getting lost among these islands wouldn't be a great outcome."

"Lost? Me? Are you questioning my leadership again?" Her voice grew louder with every word.

I backed away from her anger. "No, no, of course not. I guess I'd thought with the way we were going to have to move through the islands, it would be easy to lose our way. Sorry to upset you."

"You didn't." She paddled to the front of the canoes. Paige and I watched from the rear. "Follow me, girls. We will wind in and out of these islands to block the waves."

The girls cheered and began paddling again. We followed, darting nervous glances at the shoreline on our left—until it disappeared over the horizon. "Uh-oh. Lord help us," I prayed. I turned and looked at Paige. She paled—lips quivered.

For the next hour, we battled wind and waves, zigzagging in and out of the islands. The girls laughed and sang, oblivious of our steady migration north. Daisy chattered with her partner, Delma—choosing the route with little care.

Noting that the canoe-train was lagging, I called, "Daisy, can we rest on the other side of this island?"

"Sure." Her faint answer came back.

"Man, this island must be huge. It's taking a long time to get around it," said Paige.

"Sure is—I bet it's a kilometer wide."

It took thirty minutes for everyone to gather on the north side of the island.

Madge threw down her paddle, bending forward. Groans sounded all around.

Suddenly, Courtney squealed in delight. Everyone sat bolt upright.

“Is that our campsite, Daisy?” She pointed to a distant shore, straight ahead. Excited chatter filled the air.

Daisy glanced ahead, then smiled. “Yep, it is. Well done, girls. We’ve made pretty good time, despite difficult paddling conditions. If you check ahead, you’ll see a break in the trees. That’s our channel. Let’s go.” We raced off faster than ever. Daisy smirked at me.

“Well, I guess my worries were baseless, Paige, but doesn’t it seem strange to you we can’t see the shoreline we were supposed to follow?”

“That concerns me also, but perhaps the channel is farther from that shoreline than we thought. It’s certain to be more than a kilometer away—out of sight?” Her face flashed a question. “We have no way of knowing, do we? Oh, I wish I had the map.”

“Ya, if we had the map in front of us, perhaps we could’ve tracked our position through the islands, just by counting them. I don’t know. I’ve never done a canoe trip like this before.”

“Why didn’t Daisy do that?”

“Confident, I guess. Perhaps she needed to prove something?”

“Let’s hope she made a good choice.” We paddled in silence, lost in thought.

CHAPTER TWENTY-THREE

We reached the channel, sweat dripping from faces. "We have arrived," Daisy announced. She sat in the front canoe, posed like the figurehead of a queen on an ancient ship. "This is it. The South Channel."

"There's no sign, so how do you know?" Courtney asked. She smiled a cheeky grin.

"It's clearly the opening to a channel—see the water is flowing down it. Exactly what we'd expect to see." Daisy gazed at the opening, and her smile faded, as a frown began to crease her brow.

The map was still buried in the pack. I said nothing but noted her frown.

"Hmmm, now where is that campsite? Perhaps it's just down the channel a bit?" She shrugged. "Let's paddle, girls. It will be nice to be out of the wind."

"And the sun is shining again," said Dora. Everyone was invigorated.

"It's like God's smiling at us, because we made it," added Madge. Heads nodded.

We paddled several kilometers—no campsite was seen. "Hey, Daisy, I thought this was a wilderness trip? We've passed three cottages already," said Courtney.

"And I thought this river was supposed to be fast—a whitewater river. But this river is just meandering along. In no hurry at all." Laura said.

"Hey, girls, look ahead," said Darlene. "The river is coming to an end."

"Ya, I see reeds up ahead," said Madge.

"And the water is getting shallow," said Courtney. "Hey, I'm stuck in the mud. Back paddle, Dora." Surprised squeaks were heard as other canoes got stuck. Finally, everyone stopped paddling and turned to stare at Daisy.

Daisy's face clouded. "Jantastic, we passed a man fishing at the end of his dock, behind us. Would you kindly paddle over and confirm our position?"

"Sure, Daisy—let's go, Paige." We turned around and dug our paddles into the water, heading toward the dock. Slowing down, we approached the quay. I waved. The man paused in his fishing.

"Hello there." A puzzled look appeared on his grizzled face. "Where are you girls going?" he asked.

"The French River, to practice whitewater paddling."

He put down his fishing rod and scratched his head, shuffling closer. "This is a bay of the French River, but it dead-ends just ahead. No rapids here. Are you sure you're at the right place?" He laughed, slapping his thigh.

Paige and I glanced at each other.

"You meant to paddle the South Channel of the French River? Am I right?"

"You sure are. Which way to the South Channel?" I asked in a strangled voice.

"Southwest of here." He pointed, then shuffled off, laughing as he went.

We paddled back to our group. "Oh, Lord. What are we going to do now?" The sun set. I groaned.

CHAPTER TWENTY-FOUR

As we paddled back to break the news, I scanned the shoreline for a promising campsite. I spotted an island a short distance away that appeared to be good for a campsite. "Paige, let's take a quick detour and check out that island."

"Sure, Jantastic."

We paddled around the small island and found a reasonable beach for disembarking and saw signs of a campfire ring. "Great, this will do for a campsite. Let's go back and tell the others." When we arrived back at the group, most of the girls were drooping. It had been a tough day one that was far from being over. "Daisy, can you paddle over here to join us, please?"

A puzzled expression flitted across her face. "Sure, Jantastic, I guess you're tired?" They paddled over and rafted with us. "What's up? What did he say?" She leaned forward—eyes full of hope.

"Nothing good, I'm afraid." I took a deep breath and blew it out. I blurted, "We are at the wrong place. This is a small side channel of the French River that dead-ends up ahead. He figures our channel is southwest of here." I grimaced, looking at the darkening sky.

Daisy stared—hope evaporating.

"On the bright side, I discovered an island just back a little way that will do as a campsite for tonight." Putting my thumbs up, I grinned.

In a small voice, she said, "I need to get the map. Paddle over to the girls and keep them occupied. Please don't tell—I will." She began rummaging in her sack. We paddled back to the group.

"What now, Lord? It's going to be dark soon, and we don't know where we're going to camp," I prayed.

"God goes before you. He knew this was going to happen. At the right time, he'll show his will. Trust now—and keep trusting. Do your part in teaching these girls to trust. Live it—by being at peace," said Little Voice.

I smiled. The girls greeted me, bombarding me with questions.

"Where's the campsite, Jantastic?"

"Did you see the rapids?"

"Are they huge?"

Soon, they noticed I wasn't answering. The questions died off. Finally, Dora asked, "Why isn't Daisy coming?" They spotted her leaning over the map, deep in thought.

"There's been a little hiccup, girls. Daisy is working it out. In the meantime, what did you think of our canoe train—did it work?"

The girls looked at each other and shrugged.

Courtney said, "Yes, worked, though it would have been easier if we had all had paddles."

"I noticed when we weren't being buffeted by the wind that the canoe-train paddled in a nice straight line," I said.

"Not at first, we didn't, said Dora. "We were the first motor team, and it seemed that no matter how hard we paddled we couldn't make much headway. The whole thing was pretty frustrating."

"I didn't hear any screams."

Each of the girls shrugged.

"What good would that have done?" said Darlene. "Instead, we stopped paddling and put our heads together to solve the problem."

"I even prayed," added Madge.

"What was the outcome?" I sat forward—so did the rest of the girls.

"We learned that if the motor paddlers both paddled on the same side and the caboose," she grinned at the word, "paddled on the opposite side, then we no longer zigzagged. We could even keep up with the rest of the canoes."

"Great thinking. Did Team Two come up with a different technique?"

"We didn't have to because Team One shared their method." The girls beamed at one another.

"Leaving the paddle behind was part of the plan," said Little Voice. *"Just wait and see how much this will help you."*

I was shocked. I realized just how proud the girls felt in overcoming a difficulty. "I've just remembered a verse that speaks about this sort of situation. It's found in Romans 8, verse 28. It says; 'God works all things together for the good of those who love him, who are called according to his purpose.' What this means is that God has used the lost paddle as a way of helping us grow. We all learned to trust him today." Murmurs of "Praise the Lord," and "Thank you, Jesus," drifted back to me. Then Daisy paddled over to join us.

"Hey, Daisy," said Courtney, who was bouncing for joy, "we've just learned that God actually planned for our paddle to go missing so that we could learn something."

"And what did you learn?" asked Daisy.

"We learned that all things work together for good," quoted Darlene. "We found out we could work out a problem together. I figure that God gave us the idea." All the girls nodded in agreement.

I watched Daisy, closely. Hearing this, she visibly relaxed.

"Okay, Lord, you led the way into this next difficult moment. Now, lead Daisy out of it."

"Good prayer," said Little Voice.

CHAPTER TWENTY-FIVE

"That was an important lesson to learn—brace yourselves for the next one." Daisy paused to glance at the startled faces. "This is not the South Channel of the French River." A shock wave swept through the group. Every eye was riveted on Daisy.

"But you told us you knew the way, that it was easy?" whispered Dora.

"I trusted you," said Georgie.

"Me too," others said.

Darlene started crying. She was not alone. Despair hit the group like a sledgehammer.

Madge threw down her paddle. "Good grief—what next?"

Daisy held up her hand. "Girls, do you remember what happened earlier today when we found out that we had forgotten the tents and a paddle?"

"Yes, it was awful," said Jane. "Everyone blamed everyone else—very nasty."

"At first—but it stopped. Why?"

The girls grew thoughtful.

"We prayed?" said Dora.

"Why did that work?" I asked.

"Our attitude changed?" said Darlene, eyes shining.

"I think so," I said. "Remember the lesson of the canoe train."

Girls looked up.

"Come on, gang. God helped us to conquer that, so he can help us with this," said Jane. Smiles reappeared.

"Let's pray," said Daisy. She squeezed her eyes shut. "I apologize for leading you astray—not my plan."

"Maybe it was God's?" said Jane.

"Anyway, it wasn't your fault, Daisy," said Courtney. "The wind was blowing us sideways."

"And you came up with the great idea of paddling in the lee of the islands," said Dora. "I don't think I could have paddled all the way without that help." Others nodded. A few more smiled.

"Who wouldn't have lost track of where we were?" said Darlene. "I bet we zigzagged around ten islands."

"It was twelve. I counted," piped Laura. The girls laughed. A new light was shining.

"Thank you, girls. I appreciate your forgiveness. Now let's see what we can do about this. I have an idea." Everyone stopped to listen.

Daisy spread out the map. "Huddle as close as you can, so you can see. This is where we are—a small channel on the north shore of the French River." Everyone twittered. "This is where we want to be—the South Channel."

"Yikes, that's a long way against the wind. But not as far as we paddled today," Georgie said.

Daisy grimaced. Then added, "We can't get there tonight."

Momentary panic reigned.

"Breath everyone—a marked campsite is here. Only two kilometers away, on the west tip of this unnamed island."

Everyone strained to see where she was pointing. "We should be able to paddle there in an hour. Plenty of time to set up camp before dark. So, pick up your paddles—let's go."

As I started paddling, I glanced around. The girls snatched up their paddles. The canoes surged forward. Phew, crisis over. So, why did I have the feeling this was not quite over? Sweat trickled down my back. I glanced at Paige. Once again, she was pale and tense. She felt it too. But what?

"Keep focused. Be anxious for nothing, but in everything by prayer and supplication with thanksgiving let your request be made known to God—and you will have peace," said Little Voice. *"Look up, little one."*

"Don't worry, Paige. God's got this."

Behind me, she let out her breath. We paddled on.

CHAPTER TWENTY-SIX

Every girl had her eyes riveted on the shoreline. "There's a beach on a small island," said Courtney.

"Sharp eyes, Courtney," said Daisy. She pointed with her paddle, so everyone could find the spot. "Follow me." The canoes turned and tagged along after Daisy.

I pulled our canoe up onto the shore. "Ah, it feels good to be standing again." I stretched, twisted, and bent over. The beach was full of groaning campers. "Okay, girls, unload your canoes and put the tents up. Does everyone know who they will tent with tonight?"

"Yes, we worked that out earlier," said Dora. Tired but happy voices filled the twilight.

"Do you want me to get the fire going or organize the food?" I asked Daisy.

"I love to cook. Would you take care of the fire, please?"

I checked around and spotted a few girls watching others put up their tents. "Hey, girls, would you help me find firewood?" Grudgingly, they rose. "I get it. After a full day of paddling, it's hard to have to set up your home, cook, and clean as well." They rolled their eyes, shuffling off. Soon the fire was crackling, and the muted sounds of campers settling into their nests floated through the night air. I sighed.

"This is a pretty nice campsite," I said, walking over to Daisy. She was sitting—dropping veggies in a boiling pot of broth. I sat down beside her to help. She was strangely quiet.

"I made such a mess of things today." Her head sank so low that her hair touched the pot.

"Hey. You can't take credit for all the calamities today. Who didn't spot the missing pack and paddle before we left?" I held my hand up. "What you can take credit for was facing up to the problems and helping with solutions. Most importantly, you showed the girls how to turn to God."

She looked up, biting her lip.

I plopped the last potato into the pot as I regarded Daisy. I stirred the embers. "We have one more problem to face."

She stiffened.

"We did not make our planned campsite." I paused. "We may not have enough time to dabble in the rapids."

Daisy gazed at the fire, then closed her eyes for a moment. "Let's check the map?"

I perked up—perhaps it wasn't hopeless.

"If I'd done that earlier, maybe we wouldn't be in this mess," she said, sadness etched on her face.

Daisy admitting an error? This was new. She had changed. I laughed as I hauled myself to my feet to fetch the map. I scurried back. "Is this where we are now?" I pointed to a circle.

"Yes, it is," she said. Stretching the map on the ground, she pointed to the map legend, which she used to calculate the distance to the real campsite. "It's less than a four-kilometer paddle to our original campsite. We should be able to paddle that in half a day, don't you think?"

"Possibly, but breaking camp always takes a while, about two hours after we've washed up from breakfast."

"The girls are well motivated, so maybe they'll move faster than normal. I bet we'll have time to paddle there, rush to set up camp, then run the rapids before dusk. We can eat dinner in the dark." She lifted her eyebrows.

"Yep, that might work—it's worth a try. But are you forgetting the canoe train—they'll be exhausted tomorrow. Slower, not faster."

Scowling, she jabbed a stick into the fire. Sparks flew—so did the pot.

I managed to grab the handle, stopping it from emptying. "Wow, we almost lost dinner." I looked in at the reduced contents.

Daisy jumped to her feet, pacing back and forth. "Great. I dumped it—but you saved some of it." Brooding, she stared at the pot. "That would've been just perfect—no dinner, no paddle, no pack, no sense of direction and no rapids. What a leader." Head hanging, she shuffled away.

"Oh, Lord, we need your help to stay positive—don't let despair take our focus off of you," I whispered.

"Remember—commit to the Lord, whatever you do and he will establish your plans. I am with you, even in the dark moments to come," said Little Voice.

CHAPTER TWENTY-SEVEN

I grabbed some extra veggies and meat from the pack and finished making dinner. Daisy had vanished. I shrugged. “Dinner is ready. Come and get it.” A herd of elephants couldn’t have made more noise than the girls. “Grab plates, cutlery, and cups from the bag, then line up for food.”

I filled every plate, and quiet munching replaced the happy chatter. I searched for Daisy. She was leaning against a tree at the edge of the clearing. I filled two plates and joined her.

Unsmiling, she watched me come. “Thanks.” She took a few bites and put the plate aside. “Sorry I deserted you.”

“It’s okay. There wasn’t much to finish up.” I gulped down half of my plate. Sheepishly, I peered up from my plate. “Aren’t you going to eat?”

“Yeah.” Instead of eating, she leaned back against the tree, closing her eyes. “Why do you think everything’s gone so wrong today? After all, we’re doing the Lord’s work, aren’t we?”

I mopped up the gravy with my bread and turned to her, nodding. “I’m not sure why. God doesn’t usually tell us.

What I do know is we are to trust. Remember our verse?" I gave her shoulder a squeeze and grinned.

"Up until now, I never knew how hard that verse is to follow. Is this how God directs our path?"

"Likely. I sense Little Voice telling me so. He directed me to a neat verse during my devotions. It said God is our refuge and strength, an ever-present help in trouble, therefore I will not fear, though the earth gives way and the mountains fall into the heart of the sea. I think it was Psalm 46. It struck me that these verses are telling me to trust God in the middle of a catastrophe. Gosh, what could be worse than the earth sliding out from underneath you and mountains falling?"

"I hadn't thought of that. You're right. There are way worse things than we've been through. It's just that you kind of feel it's your right to have things turn out well when you're doing them for God—don't you?" said Daisy. As she looked down, she spied her plate. Her stomach rumbled—she grinned and ate. "Mmm."

I headed back to the campfire. "Hi, gang, how was dinner?" Thumbs-up gestures from everyone. I sat down beside Paige. Looking around at the others, I asked, "What do you think of your first day of paddling?"

Dora piped up. "It was hard, but I feel pretty good about it. What about the rest of you?" she asked.

I surveyed the girls. Many nodded their heads in agreement—a few scowled. "Madge, you don't seem happy. What are you thinking?"

"I think someone messed up. I'm pretty ticked off about it, and my parents will be too." She sent a pointed stare in Daisy's direction. The surrounding girls ducked their heads. Others stared—mouths open.

"Hey, partner, I don't think we can blame Daisy for everything. One of us forgot the pack and paddle," said Darlene.

"I guess she isn't directly responsible, but she should've checked." Madge crossed her arms and glowered.

I could see that Madge was determined to lay blame, but her response was over-the-top. What happened in her life to make her react like that? Was this a teaching moment? *And how are we going to dig out this bitter root from Madge?* I prayed.

"Be at peace, Little One. There will be more turmoil before this is over—lessons to be learned by all. Trust and fear not," said Little Voice. A feeling of calm enveloped me. Joy shone.

The light faded from the sky. "Hey, it's time for campfire. Everyone spread out to find firewood. Many of my favourite memories are of canoe trip campfires—sitting around, stirring the embers, singing, and exchanging stories." I love camping.

"Don't forget the hot chocolate," added Paige. Smiling, she headed off for more wood.

I poked at the glowing coals. "What turmoil, Lord?" I whispered.

CHAPTER TWENTY-EIGHT

I had the snack laid out, ready to cook, and the fire glowed. I stirred the hot chocolate to keep it from scorching. Daisy joined us, bringing along an armful of thicker sticks, with the bark peeled off. She dropped them. Startled campers jumped.

Picking up a stick and examining it closely, Courtney said, "These sticks have blunt ends, so it's clear they're not for hotdogs or marshmallows." She regarded Daisy, one eyebrow cocked.

Daisy rubbed her hands together. "We have a real treat for you tonight. We're making Dough Boys."

The girls looked at each other, shrugging. "Okay, Daisy," said Delma. "What's a Dough Boy?"

"Picture a light, flaky pastry, with filling spilling out with the first bite. That's a Dough Boy, campfire style."

I licked my lips in anticipation. "Tell them about the fillings, Daisy."

Eager, hungry faces leaned forward.

"We have cinnamon, brown sugar and butter, apple jelly, Nutella, and strawberry preserves." *Yums* hummed all around.

"How do we make them?"

Daisy grabbed a stick and a glob of sticky dough, which she put on the end of the stick. “First, pick up your stick and wipe off any debris. Then, put the dough on the end, like this, and work it gently around the stick until it forms a thin dough pocket. Make sure it’s not too thick or the inside will be doughy.” She held her stick over the coals, turning it with a constant rotating motion so it didn’t burn. “Bake until it’s golden brown, like this.”

The smell of baking filled the air. My mouth watered.

Daisy stepped away from the fire with her toasted Dough Boy. “Gently ease the biscuit off of the stick.” She twisted it off with care. The aroma of freshly baked pastry made our stomachs growl. “Now, put your chosen filling inside. I like butter, brown sugar, and cinnamon.” She put a glob of butter inside and let it melt, then sprinkled cinnamon and brown sugar. “Anyone want to try a bite?” Everyone surged forward, hands extended.

“Mmm.” The girls licked their lips and fingers, then grabbed sticks and dough to make their own.

Joyful chatter filled the air. The discontentment disappeared. Soon the campers sat in clumps around the fire, sipping hot chocolate and eating Dough Boys. We spent the rest of the evening eating, singing, and storytelling. A peaceful atmosphere prevailed.

“All right, girls, toss your doughy sticks into the fire to burn away the smell. We don’t want a bear invasion of our campsite,” I said.

“Are there bears around here?” asked Darlene. She gulped, casting her gaze around the campsite perimeter.

“This is a real forest. Of course, there are bears. Plus raccoons, squirrels, martens, deer, moose, and maybe some wild cats.” The girls huddled closer to the fire. “Normally these wild animals will keep clear of humans, but all animals forage for food, so if you keep open food at your campsite or in your tent, then you can expect them to be drawn in." The girls looked over at the knapsack full of food.

"What do we do about our supplies?" asked Dora. "We don't want to burn it—we'd starve. But I also don't want to be eaten by a bear." Mumbling agreement echoed around the circle.

"Mom, come and get me," said Jane, a particularly timid camper. Everyone laughed as I tried to plug my pretend phone into a tree. "Hello, Mrs. Andrews, this is Jantastic from camp ABK. Would you paddle out here and get Jane before the bear eats her? Thank you." I pretended to hang up. "She said she'd pick you up on Saturday." I gave Jane a hug as everyone giggled.

"Now, in answer to your question, Dora, we do have to do something very special to protect us from predators and our food from foragers," I said. "When camping or canoe tripping, we hang the packs in a tree. Far enough away from our campsite that the animals will go there, not to our tents." Relieved faces shone back at me. "Okay, it's time for bed. Everyone brush your teeth, rinse your toothbrush well, and put it in a bag with your toothpaste. Add them to the top of the food pack."

"Do bears like toothpaste?" asked Courtney. "They must be starving."

"Maybe bears just like white teeth to grin at their prey." said Darlene. Everyone laughed as they headed off. Madge walked off by herself. Should I join her or leave her alone? I compromised and hovered close by.

Madge found a spot outside the circle of friends, acting like she didn't want company. Instead, she savoured her Dough Boy. The pastry oozed apple jelly and butter. Hers was way larger than mine. "Wow, she must be hungry after our busy day. Don't know how she'll eat all that, but she is a bit bigger than me." I grinned and focused on my own delicious treat.

Soon, it was time to head to bed. I told everyone to tidy up and get ready for bed. I scanned the area. Madge held her hoodie and kept glancing around in a furtive way. Eventually, she joined everyone else to brush her teeth. I relaxed, exhausted after a very busy day.

All the campers gave Daisy their toothbrushes and paste, then headed for their tents. Madge was the last to join her tent pals but stopped for a moment to hang her hoodie at the door, tucked in under the fly.

Why?

CHAPTER TWENTY-NINE

Daisy hovered over the open food pack, watching the girls dump their toothbrushes and paste into it. "Has everyone brought their stuff?" Everyone nodded. "Okay, Jantastic, let's tie this pack up. Hey, girls, go in pairs and find us a tree with a branch that's low enough to throw a rope over it."

The girls ran off giggling to do the job. "Daisy, we've found the perfect tree," called Jane and Laura. Everyone ran over to check it out. I lagged behind dragging the food pack. "Now I remember why I portage the canoe. This lump is heavy." Sweating, I dropped the pack at the base of the tree. I spied a branch five meters up. "I bet I can reach that."

I threw the rope.

It missed.

I tried again.

It missed.

Everyone laughed. "Okay, it's someone else's turn. Hey, Courtney, you're the tallest, could you give it a try?"

"Sure thing." She hurled the rope over the branch. "Ta-dah," she said, smiling.

"Good job," I said. We hauled on the rope until the pack hung high above the ground. Arm in arm, we all went back to the campsite. With loud goodnights and a few bear growls from teasing girls, everyone bedded down.

I piled into the tent with Daisy and Paige. "This is cozy, and I bet before the night is over, we'll be very glad for the extra body heat." I dragged over my personal pack and pulled out my diary. "Do you mind if I spend a few minutes writing? I write in my diary most nights—sometimes to a special friend."

"A boyfriend?" asked Paige. She winked at Daisy.

"Not quite—he's not eligible." I winked back, grinning.

"You mean he's married or something?" said Paige. She sat up, puzzled.

I laughed at their faces. "His name is Gaston, and he's a donkey." I kept my expression serious.

Daisy and Paige hid grins under their hands.

"Oh, that's nice, isn't it, Paige?" mumbled Daisy.

"I'm sure it is," she replied. They looked away until finally a little giggle burst out. Then the floodgates opened, and we laughed until tears ran down our faces.

"No, really, Jantastic, who are you writing to?" asked Daisy. "Is it a secret admirer?" She waited.

"Well, I admire Gaston, and he admires me, but it's no secret. Even my mother knows." Now they regarded me with strange looks. "Okay, I'll explain. Gaston was my pet donkey when we lived in Manitowaning, and I used to sit with him for hours, telling him all my secret hopes and wishes. When we moved, we had to leave him behind, but I missed him terribly. Mom and I decided that writing to him would fill that void. And it has." I smiled and shrugged. Most people thought I was a bit quirky, but I was used to it. Both girls laughed and said goodnight. I grabbed my diary to write a quick note.

Dear Gaston,

I can't even pretend tonight that I'm writing to my diary. I need you, my friend. It's been a trying day. I'm on a canoe trip, and we've had a rough start. We left behind a paddle and a pack, but the Lord showed us two alternative ways to make up for that. Then we had some bad wind and waves and got pushed off course, arriving way north of our destination. That caused some emotional displays, but I think we're past that now. The girls are still a bit on edge, but a good day paddling and the arrival at our original campsite tomorrow ought to fix that. This is a nice site, and I expect everyone will sleep well following the exhausting paddle today. I know I will.

Goodnight.
Jantastic

I flicked off my flashlight and snuggled deep into my sleeping bag.

It seemed like I had only been asleep for minutes when small scurrying sounds awoke me. I'd heard those sorts of noises before on my kids-only canoe trip. Some animal had invaded the campsite, despite our precautions. Impossible. "Daisy, I'm sorry to disturb you, but some critter has come into camp." Daisy sat up quickly.

"What animal? Do you know?"

"Not sure. Listen." We sat there in silence, listening for the sound. Then we heard it—a licking sort of sound, followed by quick little steps.

"What is it?" said Daisy.

"I still don't know. It doesn't lumber like a bear, nor scurry like a raccoon or squirrel. I'm going to peek outside—maybe I'll see it." Striving to be quiet, I lifted the flap, keeping my flashlight off, but ready. I drew back inside the tent, flopping backwards onto my sleeping bag. "I don't believe it. I've never seen anything like it."

"What?" Daisy raised her voice in exasperation. Then, the night erupted in screams.

CHAPTER THIRTY

I leaped out of the tent, flashlight in hand, Daisy hot on my tail. Our flashlights zeroed in on the source of the noise.

"Check this out," I said in amazement.

Across the campsite was a deer with its small antlers caught in the ropes of a tent, a blue hoodie hanging from its nose. The animal thrashed about, trying to get untangled. But it was stuck. Finally, the deer uprooted the tent pegs—pulling down the tent, dumping it onto the girls, and went leaping for the forest, still thoroughly entwined in the tent. In its panic to get away, it ran across another tent, flattening it as well. At last, the deer freed itself of the guy lines and charged for the woods, blue hoodie still draped on its nose. The yells and screams of terrified campers filled the air.

We dashed over to help the girls out of one tent. The other tent had disappeared completely.

The whole camp was awake, gesturing and chattering about the event.

Daisy went from tent to tent to calm campers down, while I looked around for the missing tent. I found it, hung in tatters in the branches of a dead tree. Clearly, we couldn't use it again. Pulling it down, I headed back to the campsite.

"I didn't know deer attacked people," a shaken Jane said.

I shook my head. "I saw most of the event, and I would say the deer did not attack anyone—just got its antlers tangled while it tried to eat something in that hoodie."

"Who owns the blue hoodie?" Jane asked.

Everyone turned to stare at Madge. "Why are you all gawking at me? Was it my fault the deer went berserk when it caught its antlers?"

"Why did it come to your tent, Madge? Was there something in your hoodie?" I asked.

"Perhaps my hoodie just smelled good?" She shuffled her feet, glancing down. "Well, all right. I did have my leftover Dough Boy in my pocket. But I hung my food outside the tent, just like you said." She pouted. "It was way too good to burn up." She stared—daring me to say something.

"Was it apple jelly, Madge?"

"Yes, how did you know?"

"Deer love apples. Well, lesson learned, let's finish putting up your tent, Jane." I bent down to help, but a disgruntled Madge grabbed my arm.

"What about my tent, Jantastic? Where is it?" she asked. Everyone turned to stare when I lifted the tattered tent up.

"Oh, noooo." Madge collapsed to the ground, moaning. "What will I do?"

Darlene and Delma hovered over her, hands on hips. "Don't you mean, what are *we* going to do?"

The other girls sat in stunned silence, then Jane spoke up. "Darlene, why don't you join us in our tent? It will be lovely and warm with you there."

Smiling, Darlene grabbed her sleeping bag and followed Jane.

"Why don't you join us, Delma, and we'll also be warm?" said Courtney.

Delma grabbed her stuff and left Madge without another word.

"Everyone else, head back to bed. That's enough excitement for one night. Goodnight." Excited chatter filtered through the night air as the girls returned to their tents.

Madge hung back, tears streaming down her face. She hiccupped. "I kn-knew I was doing something wrong, and I did it anyway. I thought I knew better than the rest of you, especially you, Daisy. I'm so sorry."

Daisy came over and gave Madge a hug. "We've all learned some lessons today, haven't we, Madge?"

"Yes, but what you did was a mistake—it wasn't intentional. What I did was on purpose. I made an extra-large Dough Boy because I felt I deserved it after such a bad day. Then, I was too full to finish it and reasoned if I hung my hoodie up, I wasn't breaking any rules. But I knew all along what was right." Shaking her head, she added, "My thoughts were all about me. That might have been a bear, not a deer, and the outcome could have been death or injury. I was so foolish." She hung her head, tears dropping to the ground.

"I forgive you, Madge. Will you forgive me for my mistakes?" asked Daisy.

"Oh, yes." She flung her arms around Daisy. "This feels so right."

"What does?" I asked.

"Asking and receiving forgiveness," said Madge. Casting her eyes downward, she mumbled, "I need to do that at home as well."

"Who do you need to forgive, Madge?" asked Daisy.

"My mom and dad have separated after a big argument. It's tearing our family apart. All over a silly purchase. Mom wanted a new stove, but Dad said no. Mom bought it anyway. It's all Mom's fault—I hate her for splitting up the family." Madge jumped to her feet, pacing restlessly.

"Did you tell her that?" I asked.

"Yes, I yelled it at her as I left for camp."

"How did that make you feel?" Daisy asked.

"Lousy."

"Would you like to forgive her now?" I asked.

"Yes, but she's not here." A deep sadness hung about her like a wet blanket, pulling her down.

"Then, give this issue to Jesus. Forgive her now and receive his peace," declared Daisy.

I watched as Daisy and Madge sat hand in hand praying together. When they opened their eyes, joy shone from within.

I whispered, "Jesus came into this world to save us and died to give us life. His love is so great he accepts us as we are but allows things to happen in our lives to help us grow. Will you remember tonight?"

"Absolutely," Madge said, beaming a smile.

"Then, the collapsed tent and lost hoodie were worth it," I said, eyes twinkling. "Besides, I will never forget the sight of that deer running away with your hoodie on its nose. Ha, ha. Now, let's go to bed in our tent, and we'll be nice and warm, as well. Right Paige?"

"Right." We had a group hug and then ducked into the tent.

"One of the many lessons of this trip. Good words—keep looking up," said Little Voice.

CHAPTER THIRTY-ONE

The morning dawned bright and clear. "What a glorious day," I said to no one in particular. "Rise and shine, everyone. The new day dawns, and we're burning daylight." I chuckled as I used Brad's phrase. However, we really did have to get moving. We had big plans for today.

"Ahh, don't make me move, Jantastic.," said Courtney. "My whole body hurts."

"I can't even move my arm. How am I supposed to paddle?" groaned Georgie.

"Did my mom arrive yet?" moaned Jane.

We all laughed.

"Okay, girls. You can stay in bed for another hour. That's about the time it will take me to eat all the mouth-watering, never-had-better pancakes Daisy is making. Say, Daisy, is that real maple syrup you have there? Yum," I said, grinning.

The girls stormed out of their tents to grab plates for breakfast. I winked at Daisy. She smiled and flipped another pancake.

"After breakfast, work together to dismantle your tents and pack your gear. Please make sure you put your packs down by the canoes. Each tent crew handles their own stuff," I added. Everyone grunted their understanding. I moseyed over to Daisy.

"So, what's the route for today?"

"Since we're already on the west point of our unnamed island, we will head southwest on a straight line to the mouth of the South Channel."

"Is that the next channel we'll come to?" I asked. "I thought I remembered seeing another one."

"The other channel is Wolseley Bay, which is where we need to paddle to on our last day. I pored over the map yesterday," she snapped in reply.

I shuffled my feet in the sand. "Are you going to keep the map handy today, so we can check out the location of the first rapids?"

Her look sent daggers through me. I cringed.

"No, I don't think that's necessary, Jantastic. We'll have lots of time to check those out once we've made camp."

I walked away, kicking a rock along as I went. About an hour later, canoes were loaded and ready to depart.

"Do you want me to take the rear again, Daisy?"

"Yes, please do."

Paige and I paddled to the rear, the canoe train immediately in front of us, so we could help. One camper started singing a paddling song. We all joined in. It seemed like yesterday was forgiven and forgotten. "Thank you, Lord, for the joyful voices this morning."

The morning wore on, but the girls kept up the pace. We rafted during lunch to save time. Everyone stretched back onto packs while we stopped. It was a nice interlude, as we floated westward together with the current.

"Girls, gather around. You've all done a great job of paddling this morning, but we have to keep up this pace if we want to be able to shoot rapids this afternoon." An energetic current ran through the campers—they nudged one another. "The next channel should be the South Channel and our campsite for the night." Everyone smiled, eager to start the last leg of today's journey. Sore muscles were forgotten.

About an hour later, an excited cry sounded from the front.

"There's the channel, Daisy. Do you see it?" asked Dora.

"Now that you've pointed it out, I do," said Daisy. "I might have missed it, because the shoreline has lots of little bays along it, making it hard to spot an actual channel. But I think you're right—look to your right, because there's the opening for the South Channel of the French River. Okay, girls, turn here." Daisy smiled with confidence.

Anticipation bubbled through the group. We followed with eagerness.

We paddled for about an hour, expecting to see a campsite beside a set of rapids, but we found nothing. "It seems like this channel is opening up into a small bay, don't you think, Paige?"

"Yeah, I agree. And did you see the cottages on the north shore? Is the South Channel supposed to be like this? I expected fast water and lots of rocks. This is pretty deep."

"Let's catch up with Daisy to see what she thinks. Keep going, everyone. I'm going ahead to consult with Daisy."

"Can we rest for a moment, Jantastic, while you do?" asked Darlene.

"Sure, pass the word. Everyone rest." Paige and I scooted to the front.

Up ahead, Daisy's canoe floated with the current while she checked the map. Worry creased her brow. We paddled alongside. "What's up, Daisy? Where's the campsite—

I'm sure we've paddled way more than a kilometer since turning."

Daisy looked up, tears glistening in her eyes. In an almost inaudible whisper she said, "Yes, we've paddled more like five kilometers since turning, because once again we're in the wrong channel."

My heart sank. I closed my eyes—this couldn't be happening again.

"I never noticed that this channel is heading due west, not south at all—the South Channel heads southwest. The direction was wrong, right from the start, but I didn't notice. I should have checked better ..." There was a pause."... And I should have kept the map out." She hung her head and whispered, "How will I tell them?"

I shivered.

CHAPTER THIRTY-TWO

"What!!!"

We had pulled up on shore, and were sitting on a rocky ledge, when Daisy told the news.

Dora threw herself on the ground, moaning. Darlene plopped down beside her, head in hands. Courtney stormed around in circles, muttering, 'I knew it'. Madge remained silent. She even smiled. Screams and tears of despair filled the air.

Daisy stood pale-faced in front of everyone. After a while, she walked away to sit by herself.

I sat watching, letting them digest the information. Now, it was time to intervene. "Girls, may I have your attention, please?" I rose to stand in front. Loud accusations, tearful pleas, and mumblings of all sorts greeted my request. "Quiet," I yelled. Silence followed, but the accusatory expressions told the unspoken saga. "Listen up, girls. This occurrence is as much of a disappointment to me as it is to you. You have paddled hard today to reach our planned destination, but it's five p.m., and we're not going to arrive there today." The chorus of groans and angry words began again. I held up my hand. The noise faded. "We're going to make camp here because it's a good campsite and everyone is tired. Now—unload the canoes, put up your tents, and stow your gear, while I get supper going."

"But Jantastic, what about shooting rapids? That's what we've paddled all this way to do. Can't we still get there tonight? It's not dark yet," asked Jane.

Mumbling sounded all around as the campers voiced their desire to continue. I liked their spirit.

I closed my eyes briefly. "What should we do, Lord? What is your plan?" I whispered.

"This is my plan," said Little Voice. *"This is an opportunity to grow."*

"Really? But Lord, these girls are too tired to go on."

"Not by might, not by power, but by my spirit, says the Lord," said Little Voice.

I was astounded. God wanted this, and he was going to use it for his glory.

"Okay, everyone. This will be a real challenge. Everyone will have to give their best—everyone will have to draw on God for power and strength. If we can do that, then we'll be shooting rapids tomorrow morning. Are you with me?"

Campers whooped, jumping to their feet, hugging each other.

"Okay, girls, I'll go and discuss this with Daisy." I found her sitting on a rock, staring at the sparkling water.

"Hi, Daisy, why don't you come back and speak with the girls? They're ready to listen to you now."

"Sure, they are. What can I say? I'm a failure as a leader."

"Daisy, I know this has not gone as you planned, but it isn't outside of the Lord's planning."

"Oh, sure, God meant us to get lost—great. I can tell the girls this is not my fault. That will go over well." She jumped to her feet and paced in front of me. "You can cut the nice words and just agree I'm a failure as a map reader and as a leader. Why, if you hadn't been along to share your 'big' ideas, we would still be camping at the parking lot, hoping to be picked up."

"That's a possibility, but it wasn't my 'big' idea. That came from God, to be exact, from the Spirit speaking to me. I learned to listen to Little Voice on my own disaster of a canoe trip. Since then, whenever I'm troubled, I pray, and Little Voice speaks to my heart and mind."

Daisy plopped down beside me. "Well, he hasn't spoken to me. He probably won't because he gave me a job to do—or I thought he did—and I blew it."

"God doesn't expect us to be perfect. He expects us to try our best, to approach the tasks in front of us prayerfully—to listen and obey. Have you not sensed him at all?

"Well, I suppose I have. I sensed he wanted me to come to camp. I sensed I needed to say yes to the director when asked to lead the outpost. But if I have been obedient, then why all this trouble?"

"I guess we need to grow. You, me, and all the campers. We grow best in trials, because it's only in those times, when we are distressed, that we listen to God."

"Well, I'm desperate now. I don't know how to face the campers. They will never again accept my leadership, and we're probably not going to get to the rapids with enough time to play. Oh, Jantastic, I'm such a let-down." Daisy put her head in her hands and moaned.

"Then, you're in a perfect place for a miracle, and God has gone before you and is gifting you with it right now."

"Just what do you mean by that?"

"Well, I prayed when you walked off, and the Lord told me it was not by our might we would finish this canoe trip but by his, but I didn't get it. So, I told the kids to make camp, and they told me they wanted to press on. God is working on these kids and us."

Daisy looked at me skeptically.

"It's true. They're waiting back at the shore for you. Come and hear what they have to say."

Daisy shrugged and shuffled back, her steps grudging.

"What's all this about?" asked Daisy, as she joined the group.

The campers gathered around her, chattering excitedly.

"Slow down, everyone, I can't hear you," she said, smiling.

"We want to go on, Daisy. Our goal is within sight, and we want to get to that campsite tonight. May we?" asked Madge.

Daisy stared, dumbfounded.

I raised my eyebrow, grinning. Daisy's face lit with hope. Glancing up, she saw the last rays of sunlight duck over the horizon. "This will be a race against the dark. Are you up to it? I don't know if we have enough time ..."

"Let's do it anyway," they shouted together.

Emotions passed over Daisy's face—doubt and fear, then as she searched the expectant faces in front of her, determination shone through. "Mount up, everyone, we're burning daylight."

They ran for the canoes.

CHAPTER THIRTY-THREE

The girls paddled with determination. We headed east back out of the North Channel, then turned south—Daisy in the lead with the map spread out on a pack in front of her. There were no islands or unexpected bays to wander into. Daisy sighed, shaking her head.

"Hey, Daisy," I said, "how far to the mouth of the South Channel?" The sun had disappeared beneath the horizon.

"Looks like about three kilometers."

"Girls, only three kilometers to go. Should we stop here, or go on?" Loud choruses of 'never giving up' assaulted my ears. I smiled. The sky was devoid of clouds, clear right up to the heavens. As the light slipped away, a full moon began to rise. "Oh, thank you, Lord, for this unexpected light."

Amazed voices sounded all around me as the girls admired the night sky. We paddled on silently, the moon casting a luminous radiance upon the water. As the day ended, so too did the wind and waves. We glided across the glassy surface of the water, barely leaving a ripple. It was a surreal, spiritual experience. I felt the presence of God guiding us. Awe glowed on the faces of the silent paddlers.

Then, off in the distance, a dull roar sounded.

"What's that sound, Jantastic?" asked Paige.

I stopped paddling to listen. I smiled. "That's the sound of rapids. We must be getting close. Let's scoot ahead to make sure Daisy has heard." We dug our paddles in and were soon darting to the front of the paddlers.

"Hey, Daisy. We've made good time. I think we're getting close. What do you think?"

"Yes, I agree, but with the shore becoming shadowed by darkness, it's hard to pinpoint where we are."

I peered around. She was right. The edge of the shore was no longer distinguishable. Nothing stood out as a landmark. All I could see was the outlines of tall trees. "Do you hear the rapids, Daisy?"

"Oh, is that what that sound is? I've never heard rapids before," she shrugged. "I expected to be able to see them." A nervous giggle escaped her lips.

"Are the rapids close to the mouth of the channel, Daisy?"

"I think they are." She shone her flashlight on the map. "Looks like they're right beside the campsite, according to the map."

"Oh my, this could be dangerous." I pictured rapids in my mind, gently sculling the water with my paddle, absentmindedly. "Most rapids I've seen have a strong current leading into them. There's often a slope to the river that tends to draw you in." I stopped sculling, leaning close to Daisy. "If we're not careful, we could end up going down the rapids accidentally, in the dark."

Daisy's face froze in terror. She gulped. "What can we do—what should we do?" She placed her paddle across the gunnels, floating quietly—thinking and praying.

"I expect the safest thing to do would be to find an alternative camping spot for tonight. Have you noticed any marked campsites on the map?"

Daisy flicked on the light and reviewed the map intently. "There's none marked, and I remember being told there was only one campsite at the mouth of the South Channel. On the south side of the Channel entrance, there's a lodge with a vast lawn, but it's privately owned." She gazed with longing toward it.

"That's on Commanda Island, isn't it?"

"Yes, that's correct—what are you thinking?"

"There is a narrow channel that cuts around that island, isn't there? Does it have any marked rapids?"

Daisy perused the map. "No marked rapids at the beginning of that channel, and it meanders away from the main flow of the river. Do you think it would be safe to search for a campsite down there?"

"Possibly, as long as we don't go too far, because Big Pine Rapids are around a bend several kilometers down that channel, and they would be even worse to go down than Little Pine Rapids. Is there an island near the entrance to that channel?"

"Yes, there is, about a kilometer from the entrance. Maybe it'll be suitable for camping, like last night's campsite. I think it's worth a peek, don't you?"

"Sounds like a good plan to me—the only issue will be that we will have to paddle back up to the mouth tomorrow, against the current."

"We'd better check these plans with the Lord," said Daisy. I grabbed her hand and gave it a light squeeze—it was shaking. We bowed our heads. "Oh, Lord, we thank you for your leading and strength today. Please lead us tonight. Amen. Jantastic, let's paddle away from the mouth and raft up."

"Good idea." Paige and I sped off. Before long all the canoes were rafted together, floating quietly, a short distance from the rapids. Excited chatter filled the air. Goosebumps rose on my neck. I looked toward the rapids and thought I could see the splashes of water against rocks. I turned to Daisy when a beam of light zoned in on us from across the mouth of the South Channel.

"What can that be?" whispered Paige.

"Not sure, but it seems like it's coming from the direction of the lodge. Hey, Daisy, can you see who's shining the light?"

"Nope, but we have to paddle that way anyway if we're going to look for a campsite down there."

"Okay, let's paddle. This current makes me nervous in the dark."

Me too, me too, me too echoed around the canoes. We separated and began to paddle once again. As we approached the southern shore, a voice called.

"Come on over," the voice yelled.

"Daisy, with this current, you'd best keep paddling—tuck into the alternative channel and wait for me. I'll go over and see what they want."

"Okay, Jantastic. Girls, keep paddling—follow me closely. We will be going down an alternative channel that cuts around Commanda Island, just ahead—this one has no rapids at the beginning." She gave a nervous giggle. The campers mumbled agreement and followed.

Paige and I paddled towards the light. When we arrived at the shore, a man was standing on a dock. We pulled up to it. "Hi," I said.

"Hi, there. I've been trying to get your attention. You girls were mighty close to Little Pine Rapids, and I was concerned you'd go over in the dark."

"Thanks for your concern. We were just floating for a moment to decide what to do. As you can see, we have arrived too late to safely camp by the rapids, so we were searching for an alternative campsite."

"Are you girls shooting the rapids tomorrow?"

"Yes, we plan to, but only the first set. We are beginners at whitewater paddling, so we are here to practice."

"Ah, good idea. But I wouldn't suggest going down this alternative channel tonight. There are all sorts of obstacles on it that you won't be able to see, as well as a decent current."

Disappointment slumped our shoulders.

He shook his head sadly. "That's the only real campsite at the beginning of the French South," he said, pointing to the north side of the channel. "That's what I was trying to shout to you, but it isn't safe to try to land at night—it's a bit of a tricky landing."

"Ah, thank you for alerting, us, now if you'll excuse me, I have to catch the rest of our group before they get too far down that channel." We began paddling but stopped dead in the water when the screams began.

CHAPTER THIRTY-FOUR

Startled, the stranger yelled, "What was that?"

"My girls are in trouble. I've got to go. Come on, Paige, let's paddle."

"Hold on, missy, I'll get my motorboat and some rope. Park your canoe here and give me a hand."

Paige and I jumped out and tied our canoe to the dock. Then we ran after the stranger. We met him halfway up the path, his arms loaded with ropes, blankets, and life jackets. We grabbed the gear from him and jumped into the boat. The engine roared into action, and we took off down the channel, the big searchlight illuminating the way. It wasn't long before we spotted the group. Yells, screams, and chaos greeted us.

"What's wrong? What happened?" asked Paige. We peered ahead and saw two canoes tipped over, jammed against some big rocks that guarded a small chute that cascaded over a beaver dam. "Oh, no."

The rest of the canoes were lined up along the beaver dam, girls clutching sticks so they wouldn't get swept over.

"We're coming, hold on," I hollered. Heads nodded and hands reached out to grab the boat as it edged in. We hauled the campers onto the boat. The four girls who'd been dumped into the water shivered uncontrollably. "Here's a blanket for each of you. Huddle close together on that seat while we flip the canoes. Daisy, is everyone else okay?"

"Yes, Jantastic, we're fine, but scared." She giggled nervously. The girls chattered with excitement.

"Ah, Mr. ..." I began, "I'm sorry. I don't know your name."

"It's James Parrel. I own the lodge," he said.

"Oh, thank you so much, Mr. Parrel. Would you be able to pull these canoes back to your dock with the boat?"

"Sure can, and I can do more than that. What I was trying to tell you earlier was that since you kids are stranded, I think you should stay the night at my lodge. My largest group cabin is empty. It's the only cabin big enough for your group. It's amazing, actually. I had a cancellation today, or it wouldn't have been available, and I would've had no place for you. Quite a coincidence, eh?"

We all glanced at each other in wonder. "A coincidence? I think not," I whispered. "Thank you, Lord."

We arrived at the dock. Paige and I jumped out so we could tie off the motorboat and secure the canoes to the dock. Mr. Parrel helped the frozen girls out of the boat.

"Head on up to the lodge with Mr. Parrel while I help the others to unload." I shone the light at the channel and could see four canoes coming my way. "Not far now, girls, you can make it."

"I'm so tired, I think I'll just sleep in the canoe," Darlene said, flopping back onto a pack with dramatic flair.

"Well, you can stay there, because I'm not portaging you," said Madge.

Drooping with weariness, the girls hauled themselves and the gear out of the canoes and tied the canoes to the dock. Everyone was headed up to the lodge when calls for help erupted ahead of us. We ran. The light revealed a body lying in the middle of the path, with Mr. Parrel bending over it.

"Quick, help me," he said. "She just collapsed without warning as we walked to the lodge. What's wrong?"

"Give me a little space, please," I said. It was Laura—our smallest camper. I bent over the still form, leaning close. I felt her cheeks and hands. She was freezing and unconscious. "Oh no, I think she's hypothermic. Quickly, let's get her inside to warm up." Several campers and Mr. Parrel picked her up and shuffled up the path to the lodge. "Come on, everyone, let's hurry inside so no one else faints." A mob of anxious girls followed close behind.

Mr. Parrel led us to a bright, warm cabin heated by a roaring fire. The campers gravitated toward the fireplace to warm up. We took Laura into a side bedroom. Mr. Parrel left to arrange accommodations, while Daisy and I stripped the wet clothes off Laura and cuddled beside her under several layers of quilts on the warm bed. Her shivering eased, and after a while her eyelids fluttered up. The door creaked open, and Jane peeked in.

"Is she okay?" she asked. She slipped into the room, carrying steaming mugs of hot chocolate. Sitting on the edge of the bed, she grabbed one of her hands. "Laura, I was so worried about you." Tears streamed from her eyes. A brief smile flitted across Laura's face as she raised a limp hand to wipe the tears away.

"Thanks, my friend."

"Here, Laura, I'm going to raise you up and give you a sip of hot chocolate," said Daisy. The cup shook as she pressed it to Laura's lips.

"Mmm, good," sighed Laura. "More, please." We grinned, relief shining from glistening eyes.

CHAPTER THIRTY-FIVE

Daisy sat with me, a little way from the girls. Sitting close, quietly pondering events. "Wow, when I think of what would have happened to us if we had landed in the water by the rapids instead of next to a lodge—well?" Daisy shivered, eyes glassy.

"Yes, God rescued us by sending Mr. Parrel at just the right time, at just the right place," I said. I peered over at Daisy with a radiant smile. "Pretty miraculous."

"Sure was, but I think you've seen God's hand at work before, am I right? You seemed quicker to discern his presence."

"Yes, I'm sure I've seen him at work on several canoe trips, so I guess now I expect his intervention, even when I don't understand why."

"Would you share another story, if devotions tonight lead that way?"

"Sure, Daisy." I put an arm around her shoulders. "Here come the campers. Let's join them." Daisy and I walked over to the gang, who were pulling up chairs close to the fireplace. The usual excited chatter was missing.

We gathered around the large stone hearth, watching the flames dart like playful imps in and out of the logs, like kids playing hide and seek. Everyone seemed to be in a thoughtful mood. The remnants of a fabulous spaghetti dinner lay strewn across the old pine table behind us.

"That sure was a wonderful meal that Mr. Parrel provided," I said. Quiet murmurs of agreement sounded all around.

"Don't you think it's funny, Jantastic, that the lodge just served us the exact same meal we had planned to make?" asked Darlene.

"Quite a coincidence, wasn't it?" I searched each face intently.

"More than a coincidence, I think," piped up Laura, who was feeling well enough to join us for dinner. She flashed a triumphant smile before ducking her head, a light flush upon it.

"What makes you say that?" asked Daisy.

"Well, let's review what's happened to us, just today," said Madge. The girls all sat forward, excitement bursting from them.

"Ya, we started out the day with a firm plan to paddle straight to our campsite at the mouth of the South Channel," said Dora.

"But we went astray again," said Courtney. All faces turned to peer at Daisy, who smiled shyly.

"Yes, we did," Daisy said, "because I was stubborn and refused to keep the map in front of me." She gave a dramatic shrug. "I have learned my lesson." All the girls burst into laughter at her woeful expression. She joined in. "Seriously, though, I would have given up then. I was so disheartened, but the Lord gave each of you the courage to want to press on to achieve our goal." Her eyes glistened. "You saved the trip." Laura and Jane jumped up to give Daisy a great big hug.

"We all somehow knew that we were to keep going," said Courtney.

"Ya, I felt a whole new strength, right when I thought I could go no further," added Dora.

"Who gave you that strength?" I asked.

Choruses of *God did* echoed around me.

"For the first time in my life, I felt led by God," said Madge. "Then trouble hit, and now, I'm not so sure." She put her head in her hands. Silence. Most of the girls stared at the fire, puzzlement on their faces. This was a question no one could answer.

"If God led us to press on, why didn't he lead us to the campsite without any trouble—is that your question, Madge?" asked Daisy. Heads nodded. "Tough question, but I think our memory verses will help us think it through. Let's review Proverbs 3:5,6. 'Trust in the Lord with all your heart and lean not onto your own understanding. Acknowledge him in your ways, and he shall direct your path.' Put up your hand if you believe this verse."

One by one, hands raised. Many raised their hands right away, without much thought, or so it appeared. Others raised hands hesitantly, after a pause. "Okay, girls, put your hands down." She pointed to Laura, the one who was slow to put up her hand. "Did you have a reason for hesitating before raising your hand?"

She gulped and shuffled her feet. "I, ah, wonder if God really directed our path. If he did, he must be pretty mean, because so many things went wrong. I almost died." She gulped. Many girls nodded their heads.

"Thanks, Laura. You've put into words what many are thinking. In fact, every time things don't go as we plan, we are tempted to feel God has deserted us or that he's pretty mean."

"But why doesn't he just answer our prayers and make things work out?" asked Georgie. "He is all-powerful, so we know he can."

"I think the answer to that question lies in the first part of our verse. 'Trust in the Lord with all your heart—lean not on your own understanding'. What does that part say?"

"It says God wants us to trust that he's got the situation all planned, even if we don't understand," said Dora. The girls looked at one another in surprise.

"So, when things go wrong, God knows and is dealing with it?" asked Jane.

"Do you remember Romans 8:28? It says, 'God works all things together for the good of those who love him, who are called according to his purposes.' What does that verse mean?"

"If all things really means *all* things, then whether it's good or bad, God is using it for our good. Is that right?" said Dora.

"I think so, but I think this would be a great time to have Jantastic tell you a story. We hope it will throw some light on how our plans and God's plans mesh together. Go ahead, Jantastic."

"It all started with shooting rapids ..."

CHAPTER THIRTY-SIX

Shooting rapids! That's what we were going to do tomorrow. The girls sat forward in anticipation.

"My family has gone on a canoe trip at least once a year for as long as I can remember. We've been on a few lake-to-lake paddles, in Killarney Provincial Park, and on some smaller lakes close to where I live. But the canoe trips I recall best are ones that involved whitewater. Whitewater paddling differs from lake paddling. The first difference is that the current does most of the work for you. All you have to do is steer around some obstacles—mostly rocks, but sometimes, overhanging trees. The second major difference is the bow paddler does the steering, because she is in the best position to see the rocks and pick a path. It's scary but wildly fun as well. I love being the bowman in rapids."

"Are the bow cuts we learned this week the strokes we'll use to steer around the rocks in rapids?" asked Courtney. She gave a nervous giggle and then hugged her knees.

"They sure are, and you all caught on to the technique well. I'm going to tell you two quick stories that will help you see how God works. As a family, we mostly paddled the Sauble River, which is close to Massey. It's a fun whitewater river, but one year my parents ventured on a trip of their own down the Spanish River, which is a much bigger, wilder whitewater river. Mom was in the bow and got to choose all the paths, but they had been paddling for years together, so Dad wasn't worried. After they were on the river for a couple of days, they came to a set of rapids called Graveyard Rapids. The normal method was to walk along the length of the rapids to discuss a probable path past all the rocks. They for sure did this for rapids with the word graveyard in the name." The girls nudged each other and giggled.

"The path they picked was an easy one. Mom told us these rapids looked like the easiest run so far. She told me how confident she was as the canoe flew down the opening V of the rapids—then zigzagged down the chosen path. When they finished the course, she turned to speak with Dad, remarking on how simple it had been. They floated down the middle of the river, happy as two ducks, reminiscing about each part of the run. As they rounded the bend in the river, the sound of rushing water pounded against their ears. They gasped in panic—a waterfall was dead ahead. With no time to head for shore, they braced themselves and plunged over."

The girls gasped and clung to each other, picturing hurtling down a waterfall.

"What happened?" called Darlene. "They didn't die, did they?" Fear was plastered on every face.

"No, but Mom said it was the longest drop of her life as they plummeted straight down. She paddled madly, trying to propel them through, until they landed with a splash at the bottom. Instead of being caught in the undertow, they were catapulted out of the waterfall, safe and unharmed, onto a sandy point just downriver. You see, it was early spring and lots of water was flowing, so it pushed them much farther than normal." I searched the faces in front of me to see if they understood—but how could they? "What do you think our family learned from that experience? Was it their plan to shoot the waterfall?"

Laughter crackled all around. What a silly question.

"No, it wasn't their plan, I'm sure of it," said Paige. "But was it God's? If so, why?"

"We'll never know for sure, but I feel this was a turning point in our family. My parents came home from that canoe trip with a clear conviction that God was alive and active in their lives. They knew tumbling over a waterfall could have ended their lives and left us as orphans. Following the accident, they spent the rest of that trip talking and praying—rededicating their lives to the God who saved them. This had a big impact on my life and the lives of my siblings. Our parents changed their focus, so we changed ours. God became a part of our regular lives—not just someone we visited on Sunday. So, was this God's plan?"

"Sure seems like it, but I'm real glad God didn't throw me over a waterfall to announce his presence," said Madge, pretending to faint. Nervous laughter flew skyward, like the sparks from our fire. Then, everyone grew thoughtful.

"Everyone seems a bit tired," I said. "Perhaps we should save the next story until tomorrow night?

Shouts of no, no, no, erupted. Laughing, I looked at Daisy.

"It's your call, Jantastic, but before we move on to the next story, I want to share a verse with you," Daisy said. "Think of it as you listen to her story. It's found in the book of Jeremiah, chapter twenty-nine, verse eleven, and it reads, 'For I know the plans I have for you,' declares the Lord. 'Plans to prosper you and not to harm you, plans to give you hope and a future.' So, in the first story told by Jantastic, not knowing God could have had great consequences, but God is merciful as well as just, so he used a waterfall to get their attention." Smiling, she winked at me. "Did God have to do other hair-raising stuff to teach you?"

We all laughed.

"Yep, he did. This second intervention had me puzzled for quite a while."

CHAPTER THIRTY-SEVEN

"On this trip, my brother was in the stern again, and I was the bow paddler. My sister was with my dad. We were on the Aubinadon River, which is close to Chapleau. Susie and Dad shot the rapids first, and Brad and I followed them. Obstacles filled this river—lots of rocks, trees, and a beaver dam—like the one that stopped us tonight."

The girls giggled.

"Seemingly, we ran into an obstacle around every bend. It was a whitewater river, so we had a decent current to carry us along. On the second day, a set of rapids lay ahead of us. We rafted up to discuss. Labrador tea shrubs and tag alders filled the shoreline, and it was pretty much impossible to walk along, so we couldn't check the rapids ahead of time. According to the map, this set of rapids would run for the next kilometer, so we decided to run them without scouting and just react to what we saw. As usual, Dad and Susie went first. Brad and I waited at the top of the rapids for them to shout the signal for us to start, but it didn't come. Instead of the 'all clear' shout, we heard grunts."

The girls tensed, huddling closer to each other and the fire. "What happened, Jantastic?" asked Paige. "Did they go over an unexpected waterfall?" Everyone waited silently. No one smiled.

"No, they didn't, but we couldn't see them, so we didn't know what had happened. We decided the only thing we could do was shoot the rapids ourselves and try to help when we got there."

"But you didn't know what was ahead," said Dora. "Weren't you afraid to go?"

"Terrified. But Brad insisted we had no other option. What do you think—did we?"

"You could have tried walking your canoe down the shoreline until you could see," suggested Madge.

"The water was too deep to walk."

"You could have waited until they called you," said Laura.

"What if they were drowning and needed help?" I asked.

"Well, what did you do?" asked Darlene. The girls sat forward, as if trying to solve the dilemma.

"We prayed."

"In the middle of the river?" asked Dora. She threw her arms into the air.

"That's right, actually on the edge of the river, while I held onto a branch to stop us from drifting downstream—we asked for help and guidance. We couldn't be more specific than that because we didn't know what to expect."

"Did you close your eyes?" asked Georgie. The girls groaned and tossed bits of sticks at her. She smiled. "Just trying to break the tension."

"We opened our eyes and headed down the river." I winked at Georgie. "When we rounded the bend, we saw Susie and Dad pinned under an overhanging birch tree. They seemed to be in pain. Susie's head was just sticking out of the water. Their canoe was filling with water and bending under the pressure. They were trapped, and we were caught in the current heading straight for them." Everyone gasped, tension evident on their faces.

"Did they die?" Madge asked in a whisper.

"No, but they were in a pickle. I managed to steer the canoe past them and the tree, and on the way by, Brad was just able to grab hold of their bow. We jolted to a stop in the middle of the current. The water pressure was tremendous, but Brad held on with God's mighty hand."

"What did you do? Weren't both canoes stuck now?" asked Dora, eyes popping.

"We prayed again. Or at least Brad did. He actually shouted out to God for help. I watched, helpless to aid him, as he held on, every muscle strained. Then a miracle happened."

"What?" the girls shouted.

"The tree broke, and the canoes floated free. Dad's canoe righted itself, and they were able to paddle the broken canoe to shore. We followed."

Everyone sat back, smiling. A happy ending always makes us feel good. But was that the end?

CHAPTER THIRTY-EIGHT

"Wow, great story, Jantastic. God is amazing," said Madge. The girls nodded.

"That wasn't the end."

"What?" they shouted.

"The power of the water had broken Dad's canoe, literally bent it in half. They were safe, but the loss of the canoe stranded us about twenty kilometers from our destination, and there was no way four people could fit in one vessel."

"Well, what sort of answer to prayer was that?" asked Dora. "What did you do? Pray again?" She plopped her hands on her head with a huff.

"Yes, that was the first thing we did. Dad prayed for a miracle, his words calm and sure. I'm not sure what we wanted to happen. Perhaps, like Jane, I wanted Mom to come get me." We all laughed. "But seriously, we needed help and asked for it, but nothing appeared to happen. Dad told us to be patient, that God would answer. Then, the oddest thing happened. We all heard Little Voice. And he gave us an idea. It had to be from God, because we all got the same idea at the same time."

"Who is Little Voice?" asked Laura. The girls were puzzled.

"Little Voice is my name for the Holy Spirit, who God has sent to believers to help us make decisions. Jesus said, 'And I will ask the Father, and he will give you another advocate to help you and be with you forever—the Spirit of truth.' Little Voice often brings Scriptures back to my mind when I need them and words of advice. When you hear a small, quiet voice in your head—listen, compare it with what Scripture says, then just do it." The girls sat and pondered this thought. Skeptical expressions showed on many of their faces.

"Let's get back to the story. What idea did Little Voice give you?" asked Courtney.

"To check the map. You see, we had never run this river before, so we were unfamiliar with the surrounding area. We had perused the shoreline and decided it couldn't be walked—we had checked the depth of water and decided the canoe could not be lined down the river, but we never considered there might be a logging road close by. And there was."

"Tell me you didn't portage those canoes through the bush, then twenty kilometers to your vehicle. Now, that's what I call a husky tripper, girls," said Daisy. She flashed a cheeky grin at me. All the campers laughed.

I smiled. "No. Sadly, we only managed to salvage one canoe. Which I did portage through the bush for about one hundred meters, because Brad didn't trust me with the map and compass. Dad and Susie carried most of the gear. When we got to the bush road, we decided we would camp for the night, then hike out in the morning. We set up the tents, grateful to be alive, and were just starting dinner when we heard engine noises. Along came a trucker on his way to a lumber camp farther up the bush road. He gave Dad a ride back to our vehicle."

"Wow, that was quite the adventure but weren't you angry about losing a canoe?" asked Darlene.

"Oh, we weren't happy about that, but overall, we were very thankful to be safe and sound." I turned to Daisy. "Would you like to pick up the discussion now?"

"Yes, thanks. Okay, girls, let's review the verses we've been studying." Number one—'Trust in the Lord with all your heart and lean not unto your own understanding, in all your ways acknowledge him and he will direct your path.'

"Number two—'Be anxious for nothing, but in everything by prayer and supplication with thanksgiving, let your requests be made known to God. And the peace of God, which surpasses all understanding, will guard your hearts and minds, through Christ Jesus.'

"Number three—'And we know that all things work together for the good of those who love the Lord and are called according to his purpose.'

"Number four—'For I know the plans I have for you' declares the Lord. 'Plans to prosper you and not to harm you, plans to give you hope and a future.'

"Now, let me ask a few questions." Daisy looked around at the expectant faces. "Does God always answer prayer?"

Dora hurried to answer. "Yes—but not always in the way we want him to. I mean, Jantastic did go over a waterfall on her kids-only trip, her parents did the same on another trip, and her dad broke his canoe—so they were stuck on the river. It makes me wonder what's the point in asking if he's not going to do what we ask?" asked Dora. She appeared uncertain.

"Tell me, Dora, does God promise to always do what you ask in these verses?"

"No," was the hesitant reply.

"Who can tell me what God *does* promise?"

"He promises he will direct our paths, that he is working for our own good—in all things, and that we can have hope. Right?" asked Laura.

"I think so—you see, many people view God as a genie in the lamp. Just call him—rub the lamp—and you'll get everything you want, but God never promises that. He promises to always be with us, especially in times of trouble, and that no trouble will come upon us that is outside of his knowledge. He also promises all things—the good, the bad and the ugly—will be used by him for our good, if we are serving him. Jantastic, do you believe God was involved in your trials?"

"Yes, I do, Daisy. At the time my parents went over the waterfall, our family was drifting—sort of sitting on the fence about God. Never committing. That all changed. Then, when our canoe broke, we were in a better spiritual place, so we prayed—believing. God allowed the event to occur within one hundred meters of a logging road that was still being used. Dad and Susie were stuck under that tree and might have drowned, but we prayed, and God broke the tree. We lost the canoe, but not my sister and Dad. And lastly, God was generous enough to send a logger down the road—just when we needed a ride. It was a day of miracles I will never forget. It has strengthened my faith and made me aware God is present and active in the lives of ordinary people."

The campers were quiet, each lost in their own thoughts.

Just then, there was a soft knock at the door. Randi dashed over to open it. Mr. Parrel entered the room. "Hi, girls, I just stopped by to see how you're doing following that awful experience." His mouth dropped open as the campers cheered. He shoved his hat to the back of his head, his puzzlement clear.

I got up. "Hi, Mr. Parrel, thanks for stopping by. As you can see, we have all recovered nicely. Will you join us for a mug of your delicious hot chocolate?" He nodded and shuffled in, taking a seat by the fire.

Georgie ran over with hot chocolate for him. He sipped it gingerly, searching the eager faces. "Looks like the food has restored your energy."

"Ya, it was great, thanks so much," said Daisy.

"Did you know it was the same meal we had planned to make for dinner?" asked Dora, eagerly.

"Why, no, I didn't. Thursday night's spaghetti night at the lodge, so we had lots of extra to share with you. Quite a coincidence, wasn't it?"

"No!" shouted the girls.

Surprise shone on his face. "Oh?"

"You see, Mr. Parrel, we think God arranged it all, like he's been arranging our whole trip," said Madge.

Mr. Parrel appeared puzzled. "So, you mean to tell me this God of yours planned all the bad things that happened to you—and you're happy about it?" He shook his head.

Daisy explained. "Oh, it's not quite like that, Mr. Parrel. We believe God uses the events in our lives to help us to grow—that he's involved in all aspects of our lives, the good and the bad."

A thoughtful look flitted across his face. He mumbled, "I could do with faith like that." He cleared his throat and rose to his feet. "Well, I'd best be going. I'll see you all in the morning. Breakfast will be at seven a.m.—is that all right with you?"

"Oh, gee, thank you. That would be great," I said. I escorted him to the door. "Goodnight." I turned back to the girls. "I think we ought to pray for him, don't you?"

We bowed our heads.

CHAPTER THIRTY-NINE

A soft knock sounded at the door. Stretching, I grabbed a sweatshirt and skittered for the door, trying not to let my feet land on the cold floor for very long. I opened the door to allow Mr. and Mrs. Parrel into the room with trays brimming with breakfast. Heavenly aromas drifted upward from the plates.

"Thanks so much. It smells delicious. What a treat not to have to cook it over a campfire," I said, grinning.

"You're welcome, dear," said Mrs. Parrel. "I hear you have a busy day ahead of you—shooting Little Pine rapids this morning and paddling to Wolseley Bay this afternoon?"

"Yes, that's the plan, but as Mr. Parrel has probably told you, our plans do not always work out." I laughed.

"You seem so cheerful about that—and the girls do too. Right, Jim?" she asked.

"Sure. Puzzled me last night when you were all so joyful," Mr. Parrel added. "It got me to thinking."

"It sure did, kept him up most of the night," said Mrs. Parrel. She hugged him fondly.

He yanked the hat off his head and fidgeted with it. "Ah, could you ... ah ... I mean if you have time, that is ..." He gave a pleading appeal to his wife.

"Jim and I wonder if you leaders could spare a few minutes to tell us more about this God that is clearly so active in your lives? You see, we've had lots of trouble—barely holding onto this lodge. We need that type of help—of faith." They stood together, shuffling their feet.

"We'd love to. Please come in and have a seat by the fire. May I offer you a cup of your coffee?" I asked. They smiled and headed for the fire. "Girls," I called, "breakfast is here, come and get it." Sounds of tramping feet filled the air. I poured coffee for all of us and ran to get Daisy.

Daisy greeted the Parrels as she joined us by the fire. I handed her a mug of coffee. "The Parrels would like to know about our God, Daisy."

"Wonderful," she said, eyes glowing. "Well, it all starts with Jesus." Daisy—the one who believed she'd been a failed leader—explained the path to salvation with the clarity of a seasoned preacher. Shaped by purpose, placed here by our God, who plans for this purpose.

"Coincidence? I think not," I whispered. "Thank you, Lord."

"I told you all those things happened on purpose," said Little Voice. *"Now, proceed with the rest of your trip. Remember to look up, remember to walk humbly. I am with you."*

I felt such confidence. I was here for a purpose—didn't Little Voice just tell me that? Hadn't I done well in leading this group? I had. Now, the only part left was to share my expertise in whitewater paddling, a skill I had ample qualifications to teach. This would be a piece of cake. Just wait until those girls saw me in action!

"Oh my," said Little Voice, *"That's not what I said. Walk humbly—that's what I said. Hello—are you listening? I'm afraid not—more training is required."*

“Jantastic,” called Daisy, breaking me out of my reverie. “Can you share that story about the waterfall with the Parrels? It will help explain how God works.”

“Sure, Daisy.” I took a deep breath, then began. “It all started with shooting rapids ...”

CHAPTER FORTY

It was nine o'clock when we arrived at the campsite at the beginning of the South French River rapids. Packing had been easy this morning, because we didn't have to stuff knapsacks or take down tents. "I wonder if we could take this lodge with us on every trip?" I said to the girls. Everyone laughed. Actually, we'd all been light-hearted and exuberant this morning. Of course, the icing on the cake was the Parrels accepting Jesus as their savior. We marvelled at how God had planned that! But now it was time to play.

The campsite was close to the entrance of the rapids. The water sped over rocks and dashed down small chutes. The river was quite noisy. We landed our canoes without any problem because we could see. I grinned. "I must say, I get butterflies in my stomach even to this day whenever I hear that sound. Are you ready for some fun?" They smiled at me, nerves straining their faces.

We pulled the packs from the canoes and gathered at the side of the river. "We're going to review the strokes—then Jantastic and Paige will give a demonstration of how to shoot the rapids," said Daisy.

"Can we pray first?" asked Madge.

"Good idea." We bowed our heads.

"Let's walk along the side of the river to pick a proposed path through the rapids. I don't believe I've ever managed to follow a path I've chosen, but it's still good to know what's ahead." We stopped at the first chute. "Check out that V across the river."

"What's a V, Jantastic?" asked Dora.

"A V is a clear pathway around a rock. You see that big rock? Beside it is a very clear V. That means there is deeper water there. Enough for us to squeeze past that rock. Now, moving along, you can see just after that nice V there is a sort of bubble ridge, where the waves curl back upriver. That indicates rocks just below the surface. You want to go around waves like that." We continued on our way, remarking on where to paddle and where not to, until we reached the end of the rapids. "This is the end of this set of rapids, but it has a new type of wave. Do you think it would be safe to go through those giant bubbling waves?"

Madge had been concentrating very hard throughout the lesson. "I'm not sure. It seems dangerous—lots of tall waves. Could those waves fill our canoe if we went through them? They look different from the waves that show rocks—bouncier."

"Good eye, Madge. Those waves are different. They are called standing waves, and they are usually, but not always, just water, not rock. Standing waves are caused by the fast water of the rapids going under the slow water of the pond at the end. Many a canoeist has made it this far, then flipped going through those waves. The water is very turbulent and can bounce you right over before you know it."

"Well, how do we exit the rapids, then? I don't see any other way out," said Darlene, biting her lip.

"We have to be careful to aim for the side of the standing waves. Not as turbulent there, and less chance of being tipped. Remember, bowmen, use your bow cut on the right if you want to go right and crossbow cut if you want to go left if you're paddling on the right side. Just set the stroke to clear the rock, then paddle straight. If you hold the 'cut' too long, you will turn sideways—and you don't want that. Stern men, your job is easy, just follow your bow," I grinned. "I know it sounds a bit overwhelming, but it won't be that hard once you've practiced. The final rule is to jump out of your canoe to free it if you get stuck on a rock. Remember, the power of the water broke my dad's canoe." With that last instruction, we walked back up to the top of the rapids. Many girls gazed at the tumbling water and shivered.

We reached the top. Paige and I climbed into our canoe to do the demo. Daisy had the girls line up along the rapids to watch. "I've never done this before, Jantastic. What happens if I can't follow your lead?"

"We'll crash against a rock and likely be pushed through by the water. If we land on a rock, jump out and help me push it off, then leap in quickly, paddle at the ready, because as soon as we're afloat, the current will carry us to the next obstacle. Just do the best you can, I'm sure you'll do fine. One thing—don't waste time staring back at what you hit, because the next rock is right in front of you and coming fast. We can look afterward. Ready?" I smiled. I loved rapids.

We took off like a torpedo, plunging down the first chute. I cut past the bubbling waves and around another rock, then flew through the right side of the standing waves. "Whoopee," we yelled in unison as we floated in the pond at the base of the rapids.

"That was a blast," shouted Paige, face glowing. "My heart may never slow down again."

"Well done. I don't think we did more than kiss a rock on our way through," I said.

"Did you see that monster flat rock hiding under the bubble wave? Good thing we didn't land on it."

"You're right about that. We would have been stuck in the middle of the flow, with deep water all around. It might have proved impossible to move. Now, signal Daisy to have the girls get into their canoes."

Paige waved and Daisy gave the thumbs up.

"Send down the first canoe," I shouted. Another, thumbs up. "Our role is to watch and rescue where necessary." We waited and watched.

CHAPTER FORTY-ONE

"Okay, next canoe," I shouted and waved to Daisy. "The next canoe team is Madge and Darlene," I said.

"Madge appeared pretty confident when we were choosing our path," added Paige.

The canoe lined up for the opening chute. Immediately, they were in a bit of trouble. Having missed the V, they had to find an alternative route. They bounced off a few rocks, but the current kept them going. They exited right through the middle of the standing waves—tipping with precarious balance but managing to keep upright. Water filled the canoe. Laughing and chattering, they went to shore to dump the water out, then rafted with us to watch the next run.

"Did you see us?" said Madge.

"Sure did, you did very well, but how did you miss the first V?" I asked.

"I held on to the cut too long," said Madge, shaking her head. "I had no idea how fast a bow-cut could turn a canoe. I know now."

I chortled.

"Here comes the next canoe. After you watch them, please portage to the top again and give one of your paddles to Dora. We can't canoe train down the rapids." They nodded and then focused their attention on the next canoe.

"Oh, no," yelled Darlene. "Did you see that? They must have hit the edge of the rock under the bubble wave, and it's knocked them way over to the right." We held our breaths as the girls maneuvered around a myriad of rocks and made it to the pond. "Phew," I said, releasing my breath. "That was close."

Everyone chattered at once as they, too, rafted with us.

"Okay, Darlene and Madge, please start back to the top."

They sped over to the portage.

The next two canoes ran the rapids with very little trouble. We all stayed to watch Daisy and Delma do their run. Delma was in the bow, since she was smaller and less experienced than Daisy. They lined up for the run, perfectly from what I could see, and plunged through the chute, dead center. From there, most of the run was trouble-free. "Okay, gang, let's head to the portage and go back to the top."

As the girls picked up the canoes, Daisy asked the group, "Did you have fun?"

Joy lit every face.

"You all did great. It's only ten o'clock. Do you want to do another run now? Does anyone need to walk along the edge and pick a path again?"

"No." Everyone got ready for the next run.

Daisy glanced around at the happy, excited faces around her and shook her head, smiling. I winked. This was a great start to the last day and a wonderful end of the trip.

Paige picked up the paddles, while I hefted the canoe. It was a Grumman canoe, made of durable aluminum. It could withstand a lot of abuse before it broke, but it was much heavier than the Kevlar canoe that I usually portaged. I struggled to get it onto my shoulders. Sweat covered my brow.

"Need help, Jantastic?" said Paige. She watched my struggles with amusement.

What was so funny? She should try this maneuver. Then she'd know how tough it was. I was doing a one-person pickup of an eighty-pound, seventeen-foot canoe. Pretty tricky. You grasp hold of the gunnels in the center of the canoe, where the yoke is. Then you pull it across your knees, close to your body—then one, two, three, you rock it and lift. If all things go well, you placed the canoe yoke neatly on your neck, without crushing vertebrae. They didn't go well.

"Do you need help now, Jantastic?" asked Paige.

I was facing backward with the yoke on my chest—very uncomfortable. I dropped the canoe. The sound reverberated loudly.

"No help needed." I scowled and faced the other way to try again.

This time, the canoe caught on an overhead branch and bounced backward. Instead of landing on my neck, it landed partway down my back. I didn't have enough muscle to move it forward. I dropped the canoe. My face was red.

Paige shuffled her feet and waited. I sighed. "Would you help me position this canoe, please?"

"Sure." Within a minute we had it neatly balanced on my shoulders, yoke firmly in place. Paige walked ahead, whistling as she went. I scowled as I made my way up the path. When I reached the top, I neatly swung the canoe down and laid it gently on the ground. I cleared my throat. "How did the portage go, everyone?" I said.

"Great, it was really easy, just like you said it would be."

I grimaced as I glanced at Paige. She looked skyward, whistling a little tune.

CHAPTER FORTY-TWO

We did another run of the rapids, and the skills improved. Everyone headed up the portage trail, chattering like little squirrels. Dora spotted something ahead and ran to investigate. "Hey, everyone, look what I've found."

It was a paddle, practically the same size and design as the ones we used. "Wow," said Darlene, "God has provided a paddle. That's so cool."

We dumped the canoes at the water's edge and trudged to the packs to have lunch. Daisy checked her watch. "It's eleven-thirty now, so I think we have time for one more run before we have to begin our paddle back to the highway bridge in Wolseley Bay. Does anyone want to shoot the rapids again?" An enthusiastic "yes" was the answer.

"Can we switch positions, Daisy?" asked Georgie. "I'd like to try being the bowman."

"The teams may switch if they want to, but make sure the bowman isn't considerably bigger than the stern man or the canoe won't steer well," Daisy said.

"That's a good idea, Daisy," I said. "Paige, would you like to try the bow? You can use my paddle if you wish."

"I'd love to." She took the paddle and caressed the smooth surface. "I'll take good care of it." I tried to smile but couldn't help gazing with longing at my precious paddle. As I walked over to the canoe to take up my new position, it occurred to me this was a questionable idea. I wasn't a very good stern man. Oh well, fake it till you make it had always been my motto.

"But it's not mine. Confess your weakness, be real. If you don't, it may lead to trouble," said Little Voice.

I shook off the uneasy feeling.

Paige and I shoved off from shore, and she lined us up with the V. We flew down the chute, perfectly, then Paige cut to go around the bubbling waves, but glanced off another, unnoticed rock. I tried to bring us around but couldn't. We went flying right at the bubbling waves and landed on the rock we knew hid beneath the surface. And there we stuck. "Jump out if you can," I yelled.

"I can't. I'll be swept away. It's too deep," shouted Paige. We had noticed that earlier. I knew it to be true.

"Okay, I'm going to make my way up to you to see if changing the weight distribution will move us." I bent in half, creeping up to Paige, holding onto the gunnels. I kneeled behind her—we rocked the canoe, but it didn't budge. "Lean with me to the right as far as you can—hold on tight." We leaned over so far that our hair brushed the water. The canoe tipped precariously, but still didn't move. "Let's try the same thing, the other way." We moved. It didn't. "I'm going to go back to the stern. Once I'm seated, move back to join me." We moved. Again, the canoe didn't.

"Jantastic, admit it, we're stuck. Should we call for help?"

I bent my head. The sound of rushing water was all around me, but inside, I became calm.

"Yes, we should ask for help, but not from Daisy and crew. From God."

Paige smiled and nodded her head.

"Would you pray for us, Paige?"

"Lord, we're stuck, but I guess you know that. I've never asked you for anything before, but I think that you've brought me to this point—like Jantastic's waterfall, to teach me you are there and I need you. Please come into my heart. I believe and need Jesus. Would you save us from this problem? Please show your might by taking this canoe off of the rocks. Amen."

Tears streamed down my face. I closed my eyes and whispered, "Oh Lord, not my will but thine. All this trouble for this one moment—God's plan."

My eyes snapped open. "Go back to the bow, Paige. The Lord is going to do a miracle." Paige made her way to the bow. "Put your paddle in the water and paddle on my mark. One, two, three." We drove our paddles through the water, and the canoe glided off the rock. I don't remember being aware of Paige guiding us through the rest of the rapids. My mind was in a whirl. We floated at the bottom, then surged to meet in the center of the canoe for a hug. Tears of joy and shouts of exhilaration filled the moment.

"You're saved?"

"Yes, I am." She gave a wide grin.

"My plans are always the best," said Little Voice.

I agreed.

CHAPTER FORTY-THREE

The rest of the trip was a blur. All the teams made it down the rapids, where they heard the great news. An exultant group finished the rest of that canoe trip without a hitch. We arrived at the pickup point thirty minutes before the van arrived. We pulled our canoes out of the water and sat on our packs to wait.

"Well, girls, what did you think of the trip?" asked Daisy.

"Amazing, fun, thrilling, hard, terrifying," were some of the answers.

I laughed. That pretty much described my feelings, too. "I want to add a few more words—humbling, educational, and miraculous."

"Why humbling, Jantastic?" asked Madge.

Daisy intervened. "I think that word could apply to both of us, Jantastic, and maybe to some of you girls as well," she said, looking around. "I'll start the true confessions. In the beginning, I thought I had to prove myself worthy of leading this trip. Canoe-tripping wasn't as much a part of my experience as it was for my 'junior'—very junior—leader, so I felt I had to puff myself up. Which I did by taking over the navigation, then pretending I could do it without the map. Well, that didn't work out very well, did it?"

Everyone laughed, casting shy glances at her.

"It could've meant a totally ruined trip. It made me angry I had messed up so bad and I stayed that way until the Spirit spoke to my heart to remind me God dislikes a prideful heart. Then, you all forgave me. This trip has changed me. Not through my good planning, but through God's."

"It's time for true confession, second act. I knew I was a better canoe tripper than Daisy, and that led to pride in my heart as well. All the things I told you about really happened—the stories and skills—but these gifts are not to be used to puff myself up. The one skill I struggled with was paddling in the stern of the canoe—you see, I'm always in the bow on our family canoe trips. So I didn't tell Paige this, and I expect it was my steering, not Paige's bow cuts, that led to us being stuck on the rock. Not admitting my weakness almost caused a disaster. Sorry, Paige. I too have been changed by God's plan."

"Well, I guess I'll add my confession to the rest of you. Needing God in my life had never occurred to me. But every week at church and every moment at camp and youth events, I pretend to belong to the Christian club. God taught me, through being stuck, that I needed to change. God's plan, God's timing, not mine," said Paige.

"And I had to learn to forgive. God dug the bitter root right out of me—now I have a job to do at home," said a meek-sounding Madge. "Pray for me, girls."

"And girls, let's not forget our troubles led directly to the Parrels finding salvation."

"Praise the Lord"—was on every lip and in every heart.

The sound of a motor caught my attention. "I see the van coming."

Daisy stood. "Before we leave here, I want you all to bow your heads and ask God to reveal to you the lessons he planned for you to learn on this trip. Then commit your way to God, because his plan is best, even if we don't understand it. His timing is best. He cares about you, and the pathway to peace in this life is to give everything—the good, the bad and the ugly—to God and let his will be done," she said. "Now, let's get these canoes loaded and head home."

Tears streamed down faces as we hugged each other. Then, working together, we packed the van for home.

Lynn Halliday is a semi-retired pharmacist and an outdoors adventurer living in Northern Ontario. She and her family have paddled in the north for over thirty years and most of the stories that she writes are based on real events. Over the years she has taught Sunday School, spoken at Christian Women's retreats, and counseled at camp. Her goal in writing is to share her faith through stories.

BOOK ONE: DISASTER SERIES

www.ingramcontent.com/pod-product-compliance
Lightning Source LLC
LaVergne TN
LVHW050634100826
845148LV00011B/1857